Iron Wolves

A Tank Crew's Journey Through WWII

Kirsten Dickson

Iron Wolves: A Tank Crew's Journey Through WWII

Copyright © 2024 Kirsten Dickson

All rights reserved.

This is a work of fiction. Names, characters, places, and incidents are either the product of the author's imagination or used fictitiously. Any resemblance to actual persons, living or dead, or

This book is dedicated to the brave men and women who served during World War II. Your courage and sacrifice will never be forgotten.

Introduction

World War II was one of the most defining events in human history, a conflict that shaped nations, tested humanity's resilience, and etched stories of heroism and sacrifice into the annals of time. Among these stories are the often-overlooked experiences of the tank crews who rolled into battle across Europe, their machines symbols of both protection and destruction.

Iron Wolves: A Tank Crew's Journey Through WWII is a tribute to these unsung heroes. It follows the fictional crew of an American M4A3 Sherman tank as they navigate the chaos and brutality of the war, from the breakout in Normandy to the final push into Germany. While the characters and events are fictionalized, every effort has been made to maintain historical accuracy, ensuring the battles, equipment, and challenges reflect the reality faced by Allied tankers during the war.

This story is not just about the roar of engines and the clash of steel. It is about brotherhood, sacrifice, and the human cost of war. Through the eyes of Jack "Boss" Harris and his crew, you will witness the camaraderie that kept them going, the fear and courage that defined their actions, and the sacrifices that left an indelible mark on their lives.

Above all, this book seeks to honor those who served. Their courage, their sacrifices, and their stories deserve to be remembered, for they fought not just for their countries, but for a future where freedom could thrive.

Thank you for joining me on this journey into the heart of WWII. May we never forget the lessons of the past and the price of peace.

Table of Contents

Chapter 1: Baptism by Fire

The muffled roar of tank engines filled the humid air, blending with the distant thumps of artillery pounding German positions. Lieutenant Jack "Boss" Harris, perched in the turret of their Sherman tank, scanned the bocage-lined dirt road through his periscope. The tall hedgerows of Normandy loomed on either side, claustrophobic and ominous, their dense foliage concealing dangers. This was no open battlefield—it was a maze of narrow lanes and blind corners where death lurked around every bend.

"Driver, hold up," Jack barked over the intercom, his voice steady despite the tension in the air. "Gunner, keep your eyes sharp. Loader, have a 'Boomer' ready for soft targets."

"Copy that, Boss," replied Corporal Mike "Deadeye" Walker, the gunner. His voice carried a cocky edge, but Jack knew it was a mask for the same nervous energy they all felt.

Private First Class Joe "Quick Hands" Martinez slid a high-explosive round into the breech of the 75mm cannon, his movements practiced and precise. "Ready to send 'em flying, sir," he called out, trying to inject some levity into the moment.

Sergeant Tom "Wheels" Anderson tapped the accelerator lightly, maneuvering the Sherman with practiced ease. "Grizzly, keep that bow gun ready," he said to Private George Thompson, seated beside him. "We're sittin' ducks if anything pops out of those bushes."

The radio crackled to life with the voice of their platoon leader, Lieutenant Parker, from the lead tank. "All units, advance with caution. Recon reported German armor in the area. Stick together—watch your flanks."

Jack acknowledged the order, gripping the radio handset tightly. "You heard the man. Stay in formation. Eyes peeled."

The column of five Shermans crawled forward, engines grumbling, their tracks grinding against the rocky path. The tension was palpable, each man in the tank acutely aware of the enemy's reputation for ambushes. Jack's tank, affectionately dubbed "Iron Wolf," took its place in the middle of the formation, the safest spot but far from invincible.

Suddenly, the serene countryside exploded into chaos. A deafening crack rang out, and the ground shook as a plume of dirt erupted near the lead Sherman.

"Artillery!" Jack shouted. "Wheels, move us off the road! Get us some cover!"

Tom slammed the tank into gear, veering into a gap in the hedgerow. The Iron Wolf lumbered into a field, flattening crops as it went. The rest of the platoon scattered, each tank desperately trying to avoid becoming a stationary target.

The radio was alive with frantic voices. "Panzer IV spotted! Three o'clock!"

Jack spun his periscope, catching a glimpse of the German tank emerging from the hedgerow. Its long barrel turned methodically toward the lead Sherman.

"Deadeye, solid shot! Target that Panzer!" Jack barked.

"On it!" Mike replied, spinning the turret toward the enemy.

The first Sherman in the formation fired, its round glancing harmlessly off the Panzer IV's sloped armor. The German tank responded with precision, its cannon firing a thunderous shot. The shell punched through the lead Sherman's turret, and the tank erupted in flames.

"Jesus Christ!" George shouted, his voice cracking as the flaming tank ground to a halt.

"Keep it together!" Jack ordered, forcing himself to stay calm.

Before the crew could process the carnage, a second explosion rocked the field. A German soldier with a Panzerfaust had emerged from the hedgerow, firing at the Sherman directly ahead of them. The shaped charge hit the tank's side armor, igniting its fuel reserves.

Through the periscope, Jack could see the crew inside scrambling. The hatch was jammed, and thick, black smoke poured out. A man tried to climb out of the turret, his face blistered and red, before a secondary explosion hurled him back inside.

"Loader, Boomer! Take out that hedgerow!" Jack shouted, his voice cutting through the chaos.

"Boomer loaded!" Joe yelled.

"Fire!"

The Iron Wolf's 75mm cannon roared, sending an explosive shell into the hedgerow. The blast shredded the foliage and sent German soldiers tumbling, limbs and torsos mangled from the impact.

"That'll teach 'em," Mike growled, already adjusting the gun's aim.

The Panzer IV, however, was still in play. It fired again, narrowly missing Jack's tank as Tom swerved hard to avoid the shot. Dirt sprayed against the hull as the round impacted nearby.

"Solid shot, Deadeye! Now!" Jack ordered.

Mike took a deep breath, lining up the Panzer in his sights. "On target… firing!"

The Sherman's cannon roared once more. The round struck the Panzer IV's turret, ripping through its armor. The enemy tank shuddered, then went still as smoke poured from its hatches.

"Good hit!" Jack shouted, feeling a surge of adrenaline.

The radio crackled again, this time with Lieutenant Parker's voice, ragged but determined. "Push forward! Keep the momentum! We're not stopping here!"

Jack nodded to himself. There was no time to mourn the loss of the other crews. This was war, and their only option was to keep moving.

"Wheels, take us forward," Jack commanded. "Let's finish this fight."

The Iron Wolf rumbled back onto the road, its crew battle-hardened in an instant, their baptism by fire complete.

The Iron Wolf rumbled forward, the turret swiveling slowly as Mike scanned for targets. The air smelled of diesel, burnt metal, and the acrid tang of cordite from the earlier skirmish. Around them, infantrymen moved cautiously along the hedgerows, rifles at the ready, their faces tight with fear and focus. The Sherman provided them with much-needed firepower, its looming presence a shield against the unseen enemy.

"Stay sharp, boys," Jack said, his voice cutting through the headset. "This bocage is crawling with Krauts. Deadeye, keep that turret ready to swing. Quick Hands, have another Boomer ready to go."

"Already loaded, sir," Joe replied, his voice steady despite the chaos.

"These hedgerows are a death trap," George muttered from his seat, manning the bow gun. "One minute it's all quiet, the next—boom, you're toast."

The tension was suffocating. The hedgerows created natural choke points, perfect for ambushes. Every rustle in the foliage, every stray sound, sent adrenaline spiking through the crew.

"Movement ahead," Mike said, his eyes glued to the sight. "Looks like a machine-gun nest, tucked in the brush, two o'clock."

Jack adjusted his periscope, spotting the telltale glint of a gun barrel poking through the greenery. "Wheels, halt. Deadeye, Boomer on that nest. Let's clear it out before it chews up our boys."

"Copy," Mike said, aligning the cannon.

The tank jerked slightly as the 75mm cannon fired, the recoil thudding through the steel hull. The high-explosive shell tore into the hedgerow, detonating with a deafening blast. Dirt, smoke, and fragments of wood and flesh erupted into the air.

"Direct hit!" Mike said, a hint of pride in his voice.

"Good shot," Jack replied, his tone clipped. "Loader, get another Boomer in there. We're not done yet."

As the smoke cleared, the infantry surged forward, taking advantage of the cover the tank provided. Their movements were cautious but purposeful, rifles trained on the path ahead.

The calm didn't last.

A sudden explosion erupted near the front of the line, spraying dirt and gore. A piercing scream followed as one of the soldiers hit a mine.

Jack swung his periscope toward the sound. The soldier lay on the ground, clutching the bloody remains of his leg. Another infantryman tried to drag him to safety, but gunfire erupted from the hedgerow, pinning them both down.

"Jesus," George muttered, gripping the bow gun tightly.

"Driver, reverse! Get us out of their firing line!" Jack shouted, his voice sharp with urgency.

Tom threw the Sherman into reverse, the tank lurching backward as bullets pinged harmlessly off its armor. The infantry scattered, diving for cover as the tank repositioned.

"Loader, another Boomer!" Jack barked.

"Loaded!" Joe shouted, slamming the breech shut.

"Target, eleven o'clock!"

Mike adjusted the turret, aiming for the muzzle flashes from the hedgerow. The 75mm cannon roared again, the shell slamming into the enemy position. The explosion tore through the foliage, silencing the machine gun.

"Scratch another nest," Mike said, his voice tense.

The infantry began to regroup, pulling the wounded man back to their lines. Blood trailed behind him, staining the dirt road. Jack watched grimly through the periscope. This wasn't just war—it was a meat grinder.

"Boss, what's next?" Tom asked, his voice low.

"Stay on course," Jack said, forcing himself to focus. "We're the spearhead. If we stop now, we're sitting ducks. Keep moving, but keep it slow. Let's give the infantry time to catch up."

The tank rumbled forward again, its tracks grinding over dirt and debris. Smoke from the recent explosions hung in the air, mingling with the sharp cries of wounded men. The Iron Wolf was unharmed for now, but the battle was far from over.

"Grizzly, keep scanning those hedgerows," Jack ordered. "Deadeye, stay ready. There's more waiting for us up ahead."

"Count on it," Mike muttered, his hands steady on the controls.

The Iron Wolf pressed on, carving a path through the unforgiving bocage. Each step forward felt like a victory, but the cost of breaking the enemy's hold was written in the blood of the men left behind.

The Iron Wolf crept forward, its engine growling as it navigated a narrow lane hemmed in by tall hedgerows. Smoke from the earlier skirmishes lingered in the air, mixing with the earthy scent of churned soil. Jack's eyes darted between the periscope and the map in his lap, trying to gauge their position.

"Feels like we're walking into a damn trap," George muttered, scanning the road ahead through the bow gun sight.

Jack keyed the radio. "All units, stay tight. Watch for anti-tank emplacements or vehicles. Keep your intervals—don't give them a cluster to shoot at."

"Boss," Mike said, his voice cutting through the static of the intercom, "we've got something ahead. Hedge break, eleven o'clock. Looks like a StuG III."

Jack swung the periscope toward the break in the hedgerow and spotted the low silhouette of the German assault gun. Its boxy turretless shape sat motionless, almost blending into the foliage.

"Confirmed. Deadeye, solid shot. Quick Hands, be ready to reload fast if we don't get it on the first hit."

Mike adjusted the turret, his hands steady on the traverse controls. The targeting sight hovered over the StuG's side armor—a weak point if they could hit it before it moved.

"Target in sight. Firing solid shot!"

The Sherman's 75mm cannon roared, its recoil shuddering through the tank. The high-velocity round streaked toward the StuG, striking its side with a deafening *clang*. A burst of sparks erupted as the shot penetrated, followed by a plume of black smoke and flames.

"Direct hit!" Mike said, a hint of triumph in his voice.

Through the periscope, Jack saw the StuG's crew scrambling to escape. The driver managed to pop the hatch and crawl halfway out before the flames engulfed him, his screams cutting through the distant din of battle.

"That's one down," Jack said grimly. "Deadeye, good work. Loader, stay sharp. We're not out of this yet."

Before the crew could revel in their victory, a sharp whistle pierced the air. Jack's instincts screamed danger.

"Driver, full reverse! Now!" he shouted.

Tom slammed the controls into reverse, the tank jolting backward as an ear-splitting *boom* echoed across the field. An 88mm shell screamed past them, slamming into a Sherman behind them. The explosion was cataclysmic, the tank's turret blown clean off and landing with a metallic thud several yards away.

"Christ almighty," George muttered, his voice barely audible over the din.

"Boss, it's an 88, three o'clock! Hidden in the treeline!" Mike yelled.

"Loader, Willie Pete! Smoke that position!" Jack ordered, trying to suppress the panic clawing at his chest.

"Willie Pete loaded!" Joe shouted, slamming the breech shut.

"Fire!"

The Sherman's cannon belched white smoke, the phosphorus round streaking toward the suspected position of the 88mm gun. The hedgerow erupted in a thick cloud of blinding smoke, giving the Iron Wolf a momentary reprieve.

"Wheels, get us behind cover!" Jack shouted.

The tank lurched backward, retreating into a nearby ditch as dirt and shrapnel rained down around them. The sound of the 88 firing again sent shockwaves through the crew's nerves, but this time the shell missed, striking harmlessly behind them.

As they huddled in the relative safety of the ditch, Jack peered through the periscope to assess the damage. He caught sight of a nearby infantry squad caught in the blast zone. One soldier lay sprawled on the ground, his torso mangled beyond recognition, his intestines spilling onto the dirt.

Joe swallowed hard, his face pale. "Jesus, that's… that's messed up."

"Keep your head in the game," Jack snapped, though his voice betrayed his own unease. "We can't help them. Focus on getting us through this alive."

The radio crackled with frantic voices as other Sherman crews reported their positions and tried to coordinate a counterattack.

"Deadeye, stay on that smoke cloud. If that 88 fires again, find it and take it out," Jack ordered.

"Copy that," Mike replied, his hands steady as he scanned the treeline.

"Loader, solid shot. We're gonna need to punch through once we've got the position."

"Solid shot ready!" Joe called back, forcing himself to focus.

The crew braced themselves for the next move. The Iron Wolf was battered but still in the fight, and as long as their tank kept moving, so would their resolve. The field around them was a hellscape, but they had their first kill—a testament to their grit and determination.

Jack clenched his jaw. "Let's finish this fight."

The Iron Wolf rumbled along the cratered road leading into Saint-Lô, its tracks grinding over broken cobblestones and scattered debris. Smoke billowed from the shattered remains of the town, its once-quaint streets now reduced to rubble and ruin. Allied artillery had pounded the city for days, but the Germans clung to it fiercely, turning every corner into a potential death trap.

"Eyes open," Jack said, scanning the devastation through his periscope. "This isn't like the bocage. They've had time to dig in here."

"Got it, Boss," Tom replied, his hands tight on the controls. The tank rocked as it crawled over a mangled section of road, crushed bicycles and splintered wood littering the path.

Infantry moved cautiously alongside the tank, darting between the ruins of houses and storefronts. Their faces were streaked with grime, their rifles held at the ready. The Iron Wolf's hulking presence gave them a small measure of confidence, but the tension in their movements was palpable.

"Movement, two o'clock," Mike said sharply. "Looks like a fortified position."

Jack swung the periscope toward a cluster of sandbags and shattered walls. The glint of a machine gun's barrel caught his eye, followed by a sudden burst of fire that raked the street. Two infantrymen went down immediately, their bodies jerking violently as bullets tore into them.

"Loader, Boomer!" Jack barked. "Deadeye, target that machine gun!"

"Boomer loaded!" Joe shouted, slamming the shell into the breech.

"On target!" Mike called back, his hands steady on the turret controls.

"Fire!"

The 75mm cannon roared, sending the high-explosive shell streaking into the strongpoint. The explosion obliterated the sandbags and sent chunks of masonry flying in all directions. The machine gun was silenced, its crew blown apart by the blast.

"Direct hit!" Mike said, satisfaction creeping into his voice.

"Keep moving," Jack ordered. "There's more where that came from."

Tom eased the tank forward, its tracks grinding over rubble and the remains of abandoned vehicles. The streets of Saint-Lô were a maze of collapsed buildings and smoldering fires, every shadow a potential hiding spot for the enemy.

"Sniper!" George shouted from his seat at the bow gun. A crack echoed through the street as a rifle shot pinged off the Sherman's turret.

"Where is he?" Jack demanded, swiveling his periscope frantically.

"There! Second floor of that collapsed building!" George replied, pointing toward a jagged structure half-buried in debris.

The sniper fired again, the shot ricocheting off the tank's hull. Jack caught a glimpse of movement—a flash of a helmet behind a crumbling wall.

"Wheels, full throttle! Right into that rubble!" Jack ordered.

Tom didn't hesitate. The Iron Wolf surged forward, its engine growling as it plowed through the debris. The tank's weight crushed bricks and timber with ease, the sound of destruction echoing through the ruined street.

The sniper didn't have time to react. The Sherman's massive bulk rolled over his position, the crunch of bone and flesh beneath the tracks unmistakable. A smear of blood streaked the rubble as the tank emerged on the other side.

"Sniper neutralized," George said grimly, his voice steady despite the gruesome scene.

Jack didn't dwell on it. "Deadeye, keep that turret scanning. Quick Hands, be ready for anything. We're in the thick of it now."

As the tank advanced deeper into the city, the radio crackled to life. "All units, enemy strongpoint reported at the church square. Heavy resistance. Tanks move in to support!"

Jack keyed the mic. "Understood. Iron Wolf moving to engage."

The crew tensed as Tom guided the tank toward the square. The sound of gunfire and explosions grew louder with every turn, and the acrid stench of burning fuel filled the air. When they reached the square, the scene was chaos. German soldiers were entrenched behind makeshift barricades, their rifles and machine guns blazing. An anti-tank gun was positioned near the church, its barrel swinging toward the incoming Shermans.

"Anti-tank gun, twelve o'clock!" Mike shouted.

"Loader, solid shot! Take it out!" Jack ordered.

"Solid shot loaded!" Joe yelled.

Mike lined up the shot, his hands steady as he aimed for the gun's crew. The 75mm cannon fired, the solid shot punching clean through the gun's shield and obliterating its crew in a spray of blood and metal.

"Target down!" Mike called out.

The infantry surged forward, taking advantage of the Shermans' firepower to press the attack. The Iron Wolf fired round after round, demolishing enemy positions and clearing the way for the advancing troops.

As the battle raged on, Jack caught sight of a German soldier darting between the ruins, his rifle aimed at the infantry below. Without hesitation, he gave the order.

"Wheels, take us over that rubble. Clear the path."

Tom pushed the Sherman forward, its tracks grinding over the debris. The tank's bulk crushed the sniper's hiding spot, and a sickening crunch signaled the end of the threat.

The square fell silent as the last of the resistance was cleared. The Iron Wolf came to a halt, its engine idling as the crew took a moment to catch their breath.

"Saint-Lô is ours," Jack said quietly, though the cost of the victory weighed heavily on his mind.

The Iron Wolf stood amidst the ruins, battered but unbroken, a testament to the crew's determination to keep pushing forward.

The sky over Saint-Lô burned orange and red as the sun dipped below the horizon. Smoke still billowed from shattered buildings, casting eerie shadows on the rubble-strewn streets. The battle was over for now, but the sounds of war—distant artillery and the occasional crack of gunfire—remained a grim reminder that the fight was far from finished.

The Iron Wolf was parked in a makeshift tank yard alongside the remaining Shermans from their platoon. Two tanks were missing, their crews either dead or wounded. Jack sat on the edge of the open turret, his helmet resting in his lap. He stared out at the ruined town, his face grim and lined with exhaustion.

Below, George leaned against the Sherman's hull, lighting a cigarette with trembling hands. "Well," he said, exhaling a cloud of smoke, "looks like we survived our first day in hell. Anyone else feel like the Grim Reaper's got a crush on us?"

Joe chuckled weakly from the other side of the tank, wiping grime from his face with a rag. "I don't think the Reaper cares, Grizzly. He's just taking whoever gets in his way."

Mike climbed out of the turret, stretching his sore shoulders. "If that's true, then why'd he miss us? We're sittin' in the middle of a target every damn minute."

"Maybe he's saving us for something special," George replied darkly, grinning through the smoke. "Y'know, like a date with a Tiger or something worse."

Tom, perched on the driver's hatch, shook his head. "Don't even joke about that, Grizzly. I don't want to think about what a Tiger could do to this tin can."

The humor was macabre, but it helped them cope. The battle had taken its toll on all of them. They were alive, but the weight of what they'd seen—what they'd done—pressed heavy on their minds.

Jack finally spoke, his voice low and measured. "We lost two tanks today. That's ten men. Ten men who aren't going home."

The crew fell silent. Even George's dark humor couldn't fill the void left by the reality of their situation.

"We did our job, Boss," Mike said quietly. "We're still here because we stuck together. That's all we can do—keep sticking together."

Jack nodded, though the words didn't ease his doubts. He couldn't shake the feeling that their survival had more to do with luck than skill. They'd taken out a StuG and helped secure Saint-Lô, but it had come at a cost. And what about tomorrow? Or the day after? How long could luck hold out?

"You're right," Jack said finally, though his tone was hollow. "We stick together. That's how we'll get through this."

The men nodded, each retreating into their thoughts. Joe polished shell casings, his hands moving automatically. George smoked another cigarette, staring into the flickering fires in the distance. Mike wiped down the gun controls, muttering about how they'd need to be perfect for the next fight. Tom climbed down to check the tank's treads, mumbling about potential repairs.

Jack stayed on the turret, his gaze fixed on the horizon. The day had been a baptism by fire, and they'd come out of it alive. But he couldn't shake the unease in his chest—the gnawing fear that their inexperience would eventually cost them.

"We'll get better," Jack said quietly, more to himself than anyone else. "We have to."

The men settled into their makeshift camp, the night closing in around them. Tomorrow would bring another battle, another test of their resolve. For now, they clung to the fragile comfort of survival, knowing that the war was far from over.

Chapter 2: Push into France

The morning sun cast long shadows over the fields of Normandy, but the calm was deceptive. The Iron Wolf idled near a hedgerow, its crew scanning the horizon for any sign of movement. The platoon had made progress through the countryside overnight, but the Germans weren't going to give up without a fight.

"Anything out there, Deadeye?" Jack asked, his voice steady but alert.

Mike peered through the gun sight, his finger hovering near the trigger. "Negative, Boss. Just open fields and a few burned-out trucks. It's too quiet, though."

George, sitting in his position at the bow gun, snorted. "When it's quiet, you know the Krauts are up to something."

The radio crackled, breaking the uneasy silence. "All units, enemy counterattack inbound. Tanks and infantry spotted approaching from the northeast. Hold your positions and prepare to engage!"

Jack's pulse quickened. He keyed the mic. "Iron Wolf acknowledges. Everyone, get ready. Wheels, position us to cover the left flank. Deadeye, scan for armor. Quick Hands, load up a solid shot for the first target."

Tom revved the engine, steering the Sherman into position near a gap in the hedgerow. Joe grabbed a solid shot shell and loaded it into the breech with practiced efficiency.

"Contact! Panzer IVs, three o'clock!" Mike called out.

Jack swung his periscope to the right, spotting the sleek profiles of three Panzer IV tanks advancing across the open field. Behind them, German infantry surged forward in tight formation, their rifles glinting in the sunlight. A half-track bristling with machine guns rumbled alongside them, kicking up a cloud of dust.

"They're bringing everything they've got," Jack muttered. "Driver, hold position. Gunner, target the lead Panzer with solid shot. Let's take it down before they spread out."

Mike lined up the sights, his breathing steady. "On target. Firing!"

The Sherman's cannon roared, the solid shot streaking across the field. The round struck the lead Panzer IV square in its frontal armor, punching through and igniting the ammunition inside. The tank erupted in a fireball, sending its turret flying into the air.

"Good hit!" Jack shouted. "Loader, another solid shot!"

"Loaded!" Joe called back, already slamming the next shell into place.

The remaining Panzers veered to the sides, firing their cannons. One shell whizzed past the Iron Wolf, exploding harmlessly behind it, while another struck a Sherman in the rear of the column, disabling it.

"Incoming infantry!" George yelled, opening up with the bow-mounted machine gun. The .30-caliber rounds ripped into the advancing German soldiers, cutting down several as they tried to close the distance.

Jack keyed the radio. "All units, fire 'Willie Pete' to obscure their line of sight. We'll hit them hard once they're blind."

Joe loaded a smoke round, calling out, "Willie Pete loaded!"

"Fire!" Jack commanded.

The cannon belched white smoke, the phosphorus round landing in front of the advancing infantry. Thick clouds billowed out, obscuring the Germans' view and forcing them to slow their advance.

"Now's our chance!" Jack shouted. "Target that half-track!"

Mike swiveled the turret, locking onto the vehicle as it emerged from the smoke. The half-track's gunners opened fire, bullets pinging off the Sherman's armor.

"Boomer loaded!" Joe called.

"Firing!" Mike replied.

The high-explosive round slammed into the half-track, detonating its fuel reserves. The explosion was deafening, a fireball engulfing the vehicle and its occupants. Limbs and twisted metal were flung into the air, raining down on the smoldering wreckage.

"Holy hell," George muttered, his voice thick with a mix of awe and horror.

"Keep it together," Jack snapped. "They're still coming. Deadeye, stay on those Panzers!"

The remaining Panzer IVs had used the smoke for cover, flanking to the right. One fired a shot that clipped a Sherman, its track blown clean off. The crippled tank veered to the side, its crew scrambling to abandon it before the Germans could finish it off.

"Solid shot, quick!" Jack barked.

Mike adjusted his aim, targeting the nearest Panzer. He fired, and the round struck the German tank's turret, disabling its gun. The Panzer shuddered to a stop, smoke pouring from the impact point.

"That's two down," Mike said, a grim edge to his voice.

The third Panzer fired again, its round striking dangerously close to the Iron Wolf. The shockwave rocked the Sherman, but the armor held.

"Loader, solid shot! Let's end this!" Jack shouted.

"Loaded!" Joe replied, his hands steady despite the chaos.

Mike lined up the shot and fired. The round tore into the Panzer's engine compartment, igniting its fuel. Flames engulfed the tank, and its crew bailed out, running for cover only to be mowed down by infantry fire.

The smoke cleared, revealing the broken remains of the German counterattack. Burned-out tanks and bodies littered the field, the once-organized force reduced to chaos.

"All units, enemy counterattack neutralized. Regroup and assess damage," came the voice over the radio.

Jack slumped back in his seat, the adrenaline finally subsiding. "Good work, everyone. We held the line."

The crew exchanged weary glances, the weight of what they'd just survived sinking in. The Iron Wolf had taken its share of the fight, but they knew this was only the beginning. France wasn't free yet, and the war wasn't over.

The battlefield ahead was a patchwork of broken terrain, hedgerows, and hastily abandoned farm equipment. Smoke from the earlier skirmish still lingered, swirling in the breeze like a shroud over the wounded land. Jack "Boss" Harris stood half out of the turret, his eyes scanning the horizon through his binoculars. The Iron Wolf was on the move again, part of a three-tank formation working to outflank a stubborn German defensive position.

"Alright, boys," Jack called into the intercom. "This is where we earn our pay. We've got dug-in Krauts ahead, trenches and machine-gun nests. Command wants us to sweep around their flank and hit 'em where it hurts."

"Sounds like a party," George muttered, his voice dripping with sarcasm. "Just hope they don't bring more of those Panzerfausts."

"They will," Mike "Deadeye" Walker replied from his seat at the gunner's controls. "That's why we've got to hit fast and hit hard. Boss, what's the plan?"

Jack keyed the platoon radio channel. "This is Iron Wolf. All units, tighten formation. We're going wide to the left. Iron Fox, you take the right. Iron Claw, stay center and keep their attention. Move quick and stay tight. Let's show these Krauts why Shermans hunt in packs."

Acknowledgments crackled through the radio as the other two tanks in their group fell into formation. The three Shermans advanced in a loose triangle, engines growling as they maneuvered through the uneven terrain.

"Deadeye, keep that gun ready," Jack said, his voice steady. "Quick Hands, load HE for now, but be ready to swap if we spot armor. Wheels, keep us moving smooth—no stalling."

"Got it, Boss," Tom replied, gripping the controls tightly.

As the tanks crept closer to the German position, Jack could see flashes of gunfire from the trenches ahead. The defenders were dug in along a ridge, their machine guns spitting death at the Allied infantry pinned below.

"Contact, one o'clock," Mike reported. "Looks like a trench network."

Jack nodded. "Iron Claw, keep their heads down. Fox, take the far right. Wolf, we'll hit them from the left flank. Deadeye, when we get in position, I want a canister round ready for that trench."

"Canister? You got it," Mike replied, a grim edge to his voice.

Joe "Quick Hands" Martinez pulled the canister round from its rack, a heavy shell designed to turn the Sherman's gun into a massive shotgun. He slammed it into the breech with practiced speed. "Canister loaded!" he called out.

The Iron Wolf advanced quickly, using the hedgerows as cover. The rattle of machine-gun fire and the occasional crack of a rifle echoed in the air. Jack kept his binoculars trained on the ridge, watching as the defenders focused their fire on the center tank, Iron Claw, which had begun firing HE rounds to suppress the Germans.

"Almost in position," Jack said. "Deadeye, get ready. Wheels, bring us around that hill. Quick Hands, next round's another canister."

The Sherman rumbled into place, its turret already swinging toward the trench. Through the periscope, Jack could see the German soldiers huddled in their defensive position, firing blindly at the advancing Allies.

"Deadeye, fire!" Jack barked.

The 75mm gun roared, the canister round screaming toward the trench. When it hit, the result was devastating. Hundreds of metal projectiles sprayed out in a wide arc, tearing through the German soldiers like a scythe through wheat. The trench erupted in chaos—bodies were thrown backward, limbs severed, and blood painted the walls of the dugout.

"Holy hell," George muttered, his voice thick with unease. "That's one way to clear a trench."

"Don't get sentimental," Jack snapped, though his own stomach churned at the carnage. "Quick Hands, reload. Deadeye, scan for any survivors."

Joe loaded another canister round as the Sherman's turret adjusted slightly. A few German soldiers who had survived the blast were scrambling to retreat deeper into the trench. Mike fired again, the second canister round finishing what the first had started. The ridge was silent, the defenders annihilated.

"Iron Claw, Iron Fox, flank's clear," Jack said over the radio. "Trench is neutralized. Let's keep pushing forward."

The Shermans regrouped, advancing as a cohesive unit. Jack glanced back at the trench as they rolled past, the scene of destruction etched into his mind. The ground was littered with mangled bodies, blood pooling in the dirt. He didn't linger on it—there was no time to dwell.

"Boss, you alright up there?" Tom asked, his voice breaking the silence.

Jack exhaled slowly, gripping the edge of the turret. "I'm fine. Just keep us moving."

The Iron Wolf pressed on, its crew grim but resolute. The Germans had learned the hard way what it meant to face Shermans in coordinated attack, but Jack knew this was just one battle in a long war. As the tank rumbled forward, he steeled himself for whatever lay ahead.

The Iron Wolf crawled cautiously through the dense woodland, the late afternoon sunlight barely filtering through the thick canopy above. The narrow dirt path was flanked by uneven terrain, fallen logs, and underbrush dense enough to hide an entire platoon. The tension in the tank was palpable; this was ambush territory, and everyone in the crew knew it.

"Feels like walking into a bear trap," George muttered, his hands gripping the bow gun controls.

"Keep your eyes peeled," Jack replied, scanning the surroundings through his periscope. "Deadeye, stay on that turret. Anything so much as twitches, you light it up."

"You got it, Boss," Mike replied, his voice steady but focused.

The woods were eerily silent save for the rumble of the tank's engine and the occasional crunch of branches under its tracks. Jack's gut told him something was wrong—he had learned to trust that feeling.

"Wheels, slow us down," Jack said. "Let's not make it easy for them if they're out there."

Tom eased off the accelerator, the tank's pace dropping to a crawl. The other Shermans in the column followed suit, their commanders no doubt sensing the same danger.

Suddenly, a blinding flash erupted from the treeline to their right. The crack of the Pak 40 anti-tank gun followed an instant later, the sound like a hammer striking steel. The lead Sherman in the column shuddered violently as the round struck its side armor, penetrating clean through and igniting the ammunition inside. The resulting explosion lit up the woods, a fireball consuming the tank and its crew.

"Ambush!" Jack shouted, gripping the edge of the turret as the shockwave rattled the Iron Wolf. "Wheels, reverse! Get us behind that rise!"

Tom threw the tank into reverse, the tracks churning dirt as the Sherman backed up. Another round from the Pak 40 screamed past, narrowly missing them and kicking up a cloud of debris.

"Loader, Boomer! We need HE now!" Jack barked.

Joe grabbed a high-explosive shell, shoving it into the breech. "Boomer loaded!"

"Deadeye, find that gun!" Jack shouted.

Mike swung the turret, searching the treeline for the muzzle flash that had given the Pak 40 away. The seconds dragged on like hours as they waited for the next shot.

"There!" Mike yelled, locking onto the source of the attack. "Pak 40, two o'clock! Firing!"

The 75mm cannon thundered, the high-explosive round slamming into the position. The explosion ripped through the underbrush, sending dirt, wood, and bodies flying. For a brief moment, the ambush site went silent.

But another flash came from further back, followed by another deafening crack. The second Pak 40 fired, its round slamming into a tree beside the Iron Wolf. The impact splintered the trunk, sending shards of wood and shrapnel against the tank's hull with a metallic clatter.

"Boomer loaded!" Joe shouted, already preparing for the next shot.

"Deadeye, take out the second gun!" Jack ordered.

Mike adjusted his aim, his hands steady despite the chaos. He fired again, the round detonating directly on the Pak 40's position. The explosion was devastating. The gun crew was caught in the blast, their bodies torn apart by the concussive force and flying shrapnel. Through the periscope, Jack caught a glimpse of the aftermath—charred remains and smoldering equipment were all that was left.

"Target neutralized!" Mike called out, his voice tight but relieved.

"Good work," Jack said, his tone clipped. "Loader, another Boomer. We're not done yet."

Joe slammed another high-explosive shell into the breech, ready for whatever came next.

"All units, advance with caution," Jack radioed to the platoon. "The path's clear for now, but stay sharp. There could be more waiting for us."

The remaining tanks crept forward, their turrets scanning the woods for any sign of movement. The Iron Wolf rolled past the smoking wreckage of the first Pak 40, the acrid stench of burned flesh and gunpowder thick in the air.

"Hell of a way to go," George muttered, staring out through the hull-mounted gun sight.

"Better them than us," Mike replied, his tone cold.

Jack didn't respond. His eyes stayed on the treeline, his mind already calculating the next move. They'd survived the ambush, but the price had been steep—the lead Sherman and its crew were gone, and the woods were still crawling with unseen threats.

"Wheels, keep us moving," Jack said finally. "We've got a long way to go."

The Iron Wolf pressed on, its crew battered but alive. The ambush was just another reminder that every mile they gained in this war was paid for in blood.

The Iron Wolf crawled cautiously through the dense woodland, the late afternoon sunlight barely filtering through the thick canopy above. The narrow dirt path was flanked by uneven terrain, fallen logs, and underbrush dense enough to hide an entire platoon. The tension in the tank was palpable; this was ambush territory, and everyone in the crew knew it.

"Feels like walking into a bear trap," George muttered, his hands gripping the bow gun controls.

"Keep your eyes peeled," Jack replied, scanning the surroundings through his periscope. "Deadeye, stay on that turret. Anything so much as twitches, you light it up."

"You got it, Boss," Mike replied, his voice steady but focused.

The woods were eerily silent save for the rumble of the tank's engine and the occasional crunch of branches under its tracks. Jack's gut told him something was wrong—he had learned to trust that feeling.

"Wheels, slow us down," Jack said. "Let's not make it easy for them if they're out there."

Tom eased off the accelerator, the tank's pace dropping to a crawl. The other Shermans in the column followed suit, their commanders no doubt sensing the same danger.

Suddenly, a blinding flash erupted from the treeline to their right. The crack of the Pak 40 anti-tank gun followed an instant later, the sound like a hammer striking steel. The lead Sherman in the column shuddered violently as the round struck its side armor, penetrating clean through and igniting the ammunition inside. The resulting explosion lit up the woods, a fireball consuming the tank and its crew.

"Ambush!" Jack shouted, gripping the edge of the turret as the shockwave rattled the Iron Wolf. "Wheels, reverse! Get us behind that rise!"

Tom threw the tank into reverse, the tracks churning dirt as the Sherman backed up. Another round from the Pak 40 screamed past, narrowly missing them and kicking up a cloud of debris.

"Loader, Boomer! We need HE now!" Jack barked.

Joe grabbed a high-explosive shell, shoving it into the breech. "Boomer loaded!"

"Deadeye, find that gun!" Jack shouted.

Mike swung the turret, searching the treeline for the muzzle flash that had given the Pak 40 away. The seconds dragged on like hours as they waited for the next shot.

"There!" Mike yelled, locking onto the source of the attack. "Pak 40, two o'clock! Firing!"

The 75mm cannon thundered, the high-explosive round slamming into the position. The explosion ripped through the underbrush, sending dirt, wood, and bodies flying. For a brief moment, the ambush site went silent.

But another flash came from further back, followed by another deafening crack. The second Pak 40 fired, its round slamming into a tree beside the Iron Wolf. The impact splintered the trunk, sending shards of wood and shrapnel against the tank's hull with a metallic clatter.

"Boomer loaded!" Joe shouted, already preparing for the next shot.

"Deadeye, take out the second gun!" Jack ordered.

Mike adjusted his aim, his hands steady despite the chaos. He fired again, the round detonating directly on the Pak 40's position. The explosion was devastating. The gun crew was caught in the blast, their bodies torn apart by the concussive force and flying shrapnel. Through the periscope, Jack caught a glimpse of the aftermath—charred remains and smoldering equipment were all that was left.

"Target neutralized!" Mike called out, his voice tight but relieved.

"Good work," Jack said, his tone clipped. "Loader, another Boomer. We're not done yet."

Joe slammed another high-explosive shell into the breech, ready for whatever came next.

"All units, advance with caution," Jack radioed to the platoon. "The path's clear for now, but stay sharp. There could be more waiting for us."

The remaining tanks crept forward, their turrets scanning the woods for any sign of movement. The Iron Wolf rolled past the smoking wreckage of the first Pak 40, the acrid stench of burned flesh and gunpowder thick in the air.

"Hell of a way to go," George muttered, staring out through the hull-mounted gun sight.

"Better them than us," Mike replied, his tone cold.

Jack didn't respond. His eyes stayed on the treeline, his mind already calculating the next move. They'd survived the ambush, but the price had been steep—the lead Sherman and its crew were gone, and the woods were still crawling with unseen threats.

"Wheels, keep us moving," Jack said finally. "We've got a long way to go."

The Iron Wolf pressed on, its crew battered but alive. The ambush was just another reminder that every mile they gained in this war was paid for in blood.

The Iron Wolf rolled to a halt near the edge of a battered orchard, joining the rest of the platoon for a much-needed refueling stop. The terrain was uneven, dotted with craters from recent shelling. A supply convoy had parked nearby, their vehicles lined with barrels of fuel, crates of ammunition, and spare parts. The air was thick with the smell of diesel, sweat, and the faint metallic tang of blood lingering from the ambush they'd survived earlier in the day.

"Alright, boys," Jack said, climbing out of the turret and onto the tank's hull. "We've got ten minutes. Wheels, check the tracks. Quick Hands, restock the ammo. Deadeye, help Grizzly clean the turret optics. And stay sharp—this place is a bullseye for Jerry planes."

"Always with the optimism, Boss," George said, shaking his head as he grabbed a rag and climbed onto the bow gun. "Feels like we're walking around with a 'shoot me' sign taped to our backs."

Jack didn't respond. He kept his eyes on the sky, scanning for any sign of enemy aircraft. The Luftwaffe had been relentless lately, taking every opportunity to strike at vulnerable supply lines. He had no doubt they were being watched.

As the crew worked, a low rumble grew louder in the distance. At first, Jack thought it was another Sherman, but the sound grew sharper, more distinct—a sound he dreaded.

"Enemy aircraft incoming!" a voice yelled from the convoy.

Jack spun, his stomach sinking as he spotted three German Messerschmitt Bf 109 fighters diving out of the clouds. Their engines screamed as they descended, their guns already spitting tracer rounds toward the convoy.

"Everyone, get down!" Jack shouted, diving back into the turret.

The Iron Wolf's engine roared to life as Tom reversed the tank toward a cluster of trees for cover. Around them, chaos erupted. The first strafing run shredded the convoy's lead truck, bullets punching through the thin metal and ripping into the men unloading supplies. Crates of ammunition exploded, sending fiery shrapnel in every direction.

"Boss, what do we do?" George shouted from his seat, gripping the bow gun controls.

"Nothing we can do right now!" Jack replied. "Stay buttoned up and wait for them to pass!"

Another burst of gunfire tore through the area, this time striking a fuel truck parked near the center of the convoy. The truck went up in a massive explosion, the shockwave rattling the Iron Wolf. Flames erupted outward, engulfing the nearby men in a fiery inferno.

Jack watched through his periscope as one soldier, his uniform ablaze, staggered out of the fireball, screaming and flailing before collapsing. The scene was horrific, his charred body motionless as the flames consumed what remained.

"Christ," Mike muttered, his hands white-knuckled on the turret controls. "They didn't stand a chance."

"We're sitting ducks out here," Jack said, forcing himself to focus. "Deadeye, switch to high-explosive rounds. If those fighters come low enough, I want you to light them up."

"On it," Mike replied, his voice hardening.

The fighters looped back for another pass, their machine guns ripping through the air. Bullets struck another truck, sending its fuel barrels tumbling to the ground. One of the barrels ruptured, spilling gasoline across the dirt. A stray round sparked, igniting the trail of fuel and triggering another explosion.

"Damn it!" Joe shouted, shielding his face as the fireball roared upward. "They're tearing us apart!"

The remaining trucks began to scatter, their drivers desperately trying to escape the carnage. Allied gunners on the ground fired back with everything they had, their machine guns chattering in a futile attempt to ward off the planes.

"Boss, we've got one coming low!" Mike yelled, his sight locked on one of the Bf 109s lining up for a strafing run.

"Fire at will!" Jack ordered.

The Iron Wolf's cannon roared, the high-explosive round streaking toward the incoming fighter. It missed by a hair, the explosion rocking the plane but failing to bring it down. The pilot adjusted and fired, his rounds skipping off the tank's armor with metallic pings before he pulled up and disappeared into the clouds.

"They'll be back," Jack said grimly.

The attack lasted only minutes, but it felt like hours. When the fighters finally disappeared, the devastation they left behind was staggering. The convoy was in shambles—trucks burned, supplies destroyed, and the ground littered with the remains of men caught in the chaos.

Jack climbed out of the turret, his face grim as he surveyed the scene. The smell of burning fuel and flesh was overwhelming, and the cries of the wounded cut through the air like knives.

"Boss," George said softly, lighting a cigarette with trembling hands. "You think we're gonna make it out of this war?"

Jack didn't answer right away. His eyes lingered on the blackened remains of the fuel truck, the image seared into his memory. Finally, he spoke, his voice low and steady. "One day at a time, Grizzly. That's all we can do."

The crew worked in silence, refueling the Iron Wolf and preparing to move out. The war was relentless, and there was no time to mourn. They had a job to do, and survival meant keeping their tank rolling forward.

The sun dipped below the horizon, casting long shadows across the battlefield. The smell of burning fuel still lingered in the air, a grim reminder of the attack they had just survived. The Iron Wolf was parked under a cluster of trees on the edge of a battered orchard, its engine silent for the first time in hours. The crew sat on and around the tank, each man lost in his own thoughts.

Jack "Boss" Harris sat on the edge of the turret, a cigarette smoldering between his fingers. He exhaled a plume of smoke, watching as it mingled with the rising mist from the nearby fields. "We made it through another day," he said finally, breaking the heavy silence. "Barely."

George "Grizzly" Thompson, leaning against the hull with his helmet tipped back, snorted. "Yeah, but how many of these days do we get, Boss? Sooner or later, the Krauts are gonna get lucky."

"We're the lucky ones today," Mike "Deadeye" Walker replied, his voice sharper than usual. "You saw those poor bastards in the convoy. One bad shot, and we'd have been toast too."

Joe "Quick Hands" Martinez, sitting cross-legged on the ground with a rag in hand, quietly cleaned the spent shell casings he'd saved from earlier battles. He glanced up, his dark eyes reflecting the fatigue they all felt. "We can't think like that. If we do, we're already dead."

Tom "Wheels" Anderson tightened a loose strap on the tank's tread before settling down beside George. "Joe's right," he said. "We can't let the fear get to us. That's what keeps us alive—staying sharp."

George shook his head, flicking away the ash from his cigarette. "Sharp doesn't mean squat when an 88 decides it likes you."

"Enough," Jack said, his tone firm but not harsh. "We all know what we're up against. But sitting here talking about it isn't gonna change anything."

The crew fell silent again, the weight of Jack's words settling over them like the night itself. Joe, perhaps sensing the need to break the tension, reached into his jacket pocket and pulled out a small, worn photograph. He held it up so the others could see.

"This is my family," he said, his voice softer than usual. The photo showed a smiling woman holding a baby girl, with a young boy standing beside her. They looked happy, carefree—the kind of life that seemed impossibly far away from the blood-soaked fields of France.

"That's Maria," Joe said, pointing to the woman. "She's my wife. Been married five years now. The little one's Sofia, and the boy is Mateo. He just turned six last month."

The men leaned in, their faces softening as they studied the picture. Even George, who usually avoided sentimental moments, nodded approvingly.

"Beautiful family," Tom said quietly.

"They're the reason I'm here," Joe continued. "Every time it gets bad—like today—I just think about them. If I make it home, I get to see their faces again. That's what keeps me going."

Mike leaned back against the turret, a rare smile flickering across his face. "They'd be proud of you, Joe. You're the reason we're still rolling half the time."

Joe chuckled, tucking the photo back into his pocket. "We all play our part. I just keep telling myself that as long as we stick together, we've got a shot."

George shook his head, but this time there was no sarcasm in his voice. "Damn right we do," he said, taking another drag from his cigarette. "If anyone's gonna make it through this war, it's us."

Jack looked at his crew, their faces illuminated by the soft glow of a makeshift campfire. Despite the fear, the exhaustion, and the horrors they'd witnessed, there was something unbreakable about these men.

"We stick together," Jack said firmly. "That's how we survive. One day at a time, like Grizzly said. And when this is all over, we go home. To our families, to whatever's waiting for us. But first, we've got to make it through tomorrow."

The men nodded, their resolve strengthened by the shared moment of humanity. They weren't just soldiers—they were men with lives, dreams, and people waiting for them.

As the night deepened, the crew settled into their positions around the tank, each man finding what comfort he could in the cold, unforgiving night. The Iron Wolf stood as a silent sentinel, its steel frame a symbol of the resilience they'd need to face whatever came next.

And though none of them said it aloud, they all silently promised themselves the same thing: they would see another sunrise.

Chapter 3: The Crossing at the Seine

The air around the Seine was thick with humidity, carrying the metallic tang of nearby artillery strikes and the faint stench of stagnant water. The Iron Wolf sat idle on the edge of a hastily assembled staging area, surrounded by tanks, supply trucks, and rows of infantry preparing for the next push. A river crossing was always risky, but against entrenched German defenses, it was practically a death sentence.

Jack "Boss" Harris stood on the turret, scanning a map while balancing a cigarette between his fingers. He frowned as he traced the route. The Seine was wide here, with limited crossing points, and the Germans had fortified every likely approach.

"We're going straight into a meat grinder," George muttered from the bow gun seat, leaning back with his helmet tipped over his eyes.

"Probably," Jack replied, folding the map and tucking it into his jacket. "But if we don't cross, the rest of the advance stalls. And if the advance stalls, the Krauts have time to regroup. So we make it happen."

Tom "Wheels" Anderson tightened the straps on his seat, glancing at the assembled platoon. "They're saying the 88s are dug in on the far side. We'll be sitting ducks if the engineers don't get those bridges up fast enough."

"They'll do their job, and we'll do ours," Jack said, his voice calm but firm. "Deadeye, Quick Hands—start loading us up. Mix of Boomers and solid shot. I want options when we hit that riverbank."

Mike "Deadeye" Walker nodded from his gunner's seat. "Solid shot for armor, Boomers for bunkers. Got it."

Joe "Quick Hands" Martinez opened the ammo rack, quickly stacking shells in the ready position. The high-explosive rounds gleamed dully in the faint light, while the solid shot shells sat heavier, their dark steel tips a reminder of their deadly purpose.

"Boomer loaded," Joe called, slamming the shell into the breech. "Solid shot on standby."

Jack keyed the radio, speaking into the platoon channel. "This is Iron Wolf. Ammo prepped, ready for movement. All units, check your loads and prepare for engagement. Stay tight once we're on the move."

The radio crackled back with acknowledgments from the other tanks. The platoon leader, Lieutenant Parker, chimed in next. "Iron Wolf, you'll take the lead with Iron Claw. Iron Fox and Iron Hammer will follow and provide cover. Expect heavy resistance on the far side—88s, Panzer IVs, and infantry."

"Understood, sir," Jack replied. "We'll punch through."

The crew fell into a quiet rhythm as they finished preparations. The tension was thick, unspoken but omnipresent. They'd seen what happened to tanks caught in open ground, and crossing a river under fire was a nightmare waiting to unfold.

George broke the silence. "So, Boss, what's the plan when we get to the far side? Assuming we don't get blown to pieces halfway there."

"We move fast," Jack said without hesitation. "Keep the gun ready, stay mobile, and don't stop for anything. If we get bogged down, we're dead."

"Straightforward enough," Mike said, adjusting his sights. "Just another day in paradise."

Jack climbed back into the turret, his voice steady as he gave the final orders. "Wheels, keep us moving. Quick Hands, stay on the reload. Deadeye, call out targets as soon as you see them. Grizzly, keep that bow gun ready—we'll need it for the infantry."

"You got it, Boss," George replied, checking the action on the .30 caliber.

The engine growled to life, sending vibrations through the tank as Tom revved it to full power. The Iron Wolf was ready, its crew focused despite the looming danger.

Jack keyed the radio one last time. "Iron Wolf is rolling out. Let's get this done."

The tank began to move, its tracks churning over the uneven ground as the platoon advanced toward the river. The faint outline of the Seine came into view, shimmering ominously under the dim light of the overcast sky. On the far bank, flashes of enemy artillery signaled what awaited them.

The Iron Wolf rolled forward, its steel body prepared for the crucible ahead. The crew's grim determination was palpable—this was their mission, and there was no turning back.

The Iron Wolf rumbled toward the Seine, its engine growling as the column of Allied vehicles followed the hastily cleared dirt road. The air was tense, filled with the low hum of anticipation and the sharp bark of distant artillery. The bridge ahead—a temporary Bailey bridge constructed by engineers—spanned the wide, slow-moving river. It was a fragile lifeline in a brutal war zone.

"All units, maintain spacing and prepare for heavy fire," came the crackling voice of Lieutenant Parker over the radio.

"Eyes sharp, boys," Jack said, gripping the turret's edge. "This is where it gets nasty."

The first wave of infantry was already on the bridge, their boots clanging against the steel planks as they jogged across. Engineers worked frantically on the far bank, securing the structure while keeping low to avoid enemy fire. Behind them, flashes of movement on the opposite hill indicated the entrenched German positions.

"Deadeye, keep that gun hot," Jack ordered. "Grizzly, watch the riverbank. If anything pops out of the brush, I want it gone."

"Got it, Boss," George replied, his finger twitching over the bow gun trigger.

Before the column could fully reach the crossing, the first shell struck. A deafening explosion rocked the air as German artillery zeroed in on the bridge, sending a plume of dirt and debris skyward. The infantry on the bridge scrambled, some diving to the ground, others frozen in terror.

"Artillery! They've got the range!" Jack shouted. "Wheels, full throttle—get us across before we're sitting ducks!"

The Iron Wolf roared forward, its tracks grinding against the gravel road as it approached the bridge. Another shell exploded nearby, sending shards of metal ricocheting off the tank's hull.

"They're walking it in!" George yelled. "They're gonna hit the bridge any second!"

Jack's stomach twisted as he glanced through the periscope. The German bunkers on the far side were spitting fire, their machine guns raking the riverbank. To make matters worse, a second artillery battery opened up, this time aiming directly at the bridge.

The Iron Wolf charged onto the steel structure, the clanging of its treads drowned out by the chaos. The bridge swayed under the weight of the tanks and trucks, each explosion shaking it further. Infantry ran alongside the column, their faces pale with fear.

"Target those bunkers!" Jack barked. "Deadeye, Boomer! Take 'em out!"

"Boomer loaded!" Joe shouted.

"On target!" Mike replied, swiveling the turret toward a concrete pillbox on the far bank.

The Sherman's 75mm cannon roared, the high-explosive round streaking across the river and slamming into the bunker. The explosion was massive, chunks of concrete and dirt erupting into the air as the position was obliterated.

"Direct hit!" Mike called out.

"Loader, another Boomer!" Jack ordered.

As Joe worked frantically to reload, the unthinkable happened. A German shell struck the middle of the bridge with pinpoint accuracy, detonating with a thunderous crack. The explosion tore through the structure, ripping apart its supports. The bridge groaned under the strain, and then, with a sickening lurch, it began to collapse.

Jack watched in horror as dozens of soldiers and vehicles plunged into the river below. The sound of men screaming mixed with the metallic screech of twisting steel. A supply truck hit the water nose-first, its cargo spilling out as it sank. Soldiers flailed desperately in the current, weighed down by their gear.

"Jesus," George muttered, his voice barely audible. "They didn't have a chance."

"Keep us moving!" Jack shouted, forcing himself to focus. "Wheels, get us to the far side—now!"

Tom pushed the Sherman to its limits, the tank surging forward as the remaining section of the bridge buckled beneath them. The Iron Wolf reached the far bank just as another explosion sent more debris raining down.

"Deadeye, hit that other bunker!" Jack ordered, his voice cutting through the chaos.

Mike lined up the shot, the cannon firing again. The round slammed into the second bunker, its occupants vaporized in the blast. Smoke and flames poured from the structure, silencing its guns for good.

The Iron Wolf pulled off the road, taking cover behind a shattered tree line. The crew sat in stunned silence for a moment, the sounds of battle still raging around them. Jack glanced back toward the river. The collapsed bridge was now a scene of utter devastation, the water churned with debris and bodies.

"Quick Hands, reload," Jack said, his voice tight. "We've still got work to do."

Joe nodded, sliding another high-explosive shell into the breech. The crew had no time to grieve or process what they had just witnessed. The only way forward was through the chaos, and they were still in the fight.

"Let's finish this," Jack muttered, gripping the turret controls. The Iron Wolf roared back into action, its crew determined to survive the nightmare unfolding around them.

The Iron Wolf sat at the edge of a muddy, cratered field just beyond the riverbank. The chaos of the bridge collapse still hung over the men, but there was no time to dwell on the dead or the destruction. A path forward had to be carved, and the platoon's job was to lead the way. Infantry units moved cautiously ahead, crouched low as they scoured the ground for mines hidden among the debris and churned earth.

"Alright, boys," Jack said, his voice crackling through the intercom. "We're the hammer. Stay sharp and cover the infantry. Grizzly, keep your eyes on the tree line—anything moves, I want it gone."

"On it," George replied, gripping the bow gun's controls.

"Deadeye, load up a shotgun round," Jack continued. "If we see a nest, I want it shredded before they can blink."

"Shotgun loaded," Joe called, slamming the shell into place. The canister round, filled with hundreds of steel balls, turned the Sherman's cannon into a devastating close-range weapon.

The infantry worked methodically, probing the ground with long metal rods while others watched for enemy movement. Every step forward was a gamble, and the tension was palpable.

"Boss, I don't like this," Tom muttered from the driver's seat. "Feels too quiet. They've got to be watching us."

"They are," Jack replied grimly. "Stay ready. They'll hit us the second they think they have the advantage."

Suddenly, the sharp crack of a rifle echoed from the tree line, followed by the staccato burst of a German MG42. Bullets tore through the air, ripping into the dirt around the advancing infantry. One soldier went down immediately, a crimson mist spraying as the machine gun found its mark.

"Contact! Eleven o'clock!" Jack shouted.

"I see it!" Mike called out, already swinging the turret toward the source of the gunfire.

Through his periscope, Jack spotted the MG42 nest tucked behind a pile of sandbags. The German crew fired relentlessly, forcing the infantry to dive for cover. The gun's muzzle flashed like a strobe light, its rounds tearing into the ground with terrifying precision.

"Deadeye, shotgun round on that nest!" Jack ordered.

"On target!" Mike replied, his voice tight with focus.

"Fire!"

The 75mm cannon roared, the canister round streaking toward the machine-gun position. The effect was immediate and catastrophic. Hundreds of steel balls sprayed out, shredding the sandbags and everything behind them. The gun crew didn't stand a chance. One man was thrown backward, his body crumpling like a rag doll, while another was nearly cut in half by the barrage. Blood and fragments painted the dirt, the machine gun silenced in an instant.

"Target neutralized," Mike said, his voice cold and steady.

"Good shot," Jack replied, already scanning for more threats.

The infantry began to move again, emboldened by the destruction of the nest. They advanced cautiously, their eyes darting between the ground and the horizon. A squad reached the edge of a clearing and gestured for the Iron Wolf to follow.

"Wheels, move us up," Jack said. "Grizzly, keep an eye on those trenches ahead. Quick Hands, reload another shotgun round."

"Loaded!" Joe replied, slamming the breech shut.

As the tank rolled forward, the ground beneath them felt unstable, the tracks kicking up mud and loose debris. Jack's periscope caught a flash of movement ahead—a German soldier darting from cover, carrying what looked like a mine.

"Grizzly, one o'clock! Take him down!" Jack shouted.

George swung the bow gun and opened fire, the .30 caliber rounds cutting the soldier down before he could get close. The mine clattered to the ground harmlessly as the man crumpled.

"Nice shooting," Jack said, his tone clipped. "Wheels, hold position. Infantry's clearing the rest of this sector."

The Sherman halted, its turret swiveling slowly as the crew scanned for more threats. The infantry worked diligently, marking cleared paths and neutralizing the occasional mine. The tension began to ease as the field ahead started to look more manageable.

But the respite was short-lived. Another burst of rifle fire erupted from a nearby trench, pinning the infantry down once again. Jack quickly assessed the situation.

"Deadeye, trench at ten o'clock. Give them another shotgun round!"

"On it!" Mike replied, adjusting his aim.

The cannon fired, the canister round obliterating the trench. Dirt and bodies flew into the air as the steel projectiles tore through the defenders. The few Germans who survived scrambled to retreat, only to be cut down by Allied rifle fire.

"Trench clear," Mike reported, his voice flat.

The infantry signaled the all-clear, waving for the tanks to move forward. The way was open, but the cost was evident in the bodies left behind. Jack took a deep breath, forcing himself to focus. There was no room for hesitation—they had a job to finish.

"Wheels, take us forward. Let's keep the momentum," Jack said.

The Iron Wolf rolled on, its crew grim but resolute. The field was theirs, for now, but Jack knew the next battle was just around the corner.

The Iron Wolf reached the edge of the bridgehead, its engine rumbling steadily as the crew scanned the area for any lingering threats. Smoke rose from the wreckage scattered across the battlefield—burned-out tanks, shattered bunkers, and craters gouged into the earth by relentless artillery fire. The infantry, having cleared the way through the minefield, began to dig in and secure defensive positions.

Jack adjusted his periscope, surveying the far side of the river. "Looks like they're pulling back," he muttered, spotting movement in the distance.

"Think they're regrouping?" George asked from the bow gun.

"Probably," Jack replied. "But we're not letting them get too far. Deadeye, keep that cannon ready."

"Always," Mike replied, his hands steady on the turret controls.

Through the haze of smoke, Jack spotted a German Opel Blitz truck tearing away from the battlefield. Its tires kicked up dust and debris as it sped down a dirt road, carrying what looked like a squad of fleeing soldiers and possibly supplies.

"Truck at two o'clock," Jack called out. "Looks like they're running for it. Deadeye, give 'em a Boomer. Let's make sure they don't regroup."

Joe "Quick Hands" Martinez was already reaching for a high-explosive round. "Boomer loaded!" he called, slamming the shell into the breech.

"On target," Mike said, tracking the truck through his sight.

"Fire!" Jack ordered.

The 75mm cannon roared, sending the high-explosive round streaking toward the fleeing vehicle. The shell struck the truck's rear axle, detonating with devastating force. The explosion tore through the thin metal frame, igniting the fuel tank and sending a fireball into the air.

The truck disintegrated, its occupants thrown violently from the wreckage. Bodies were flung in all directions—limbs separated from torsos, blood and viscera splattering across the dirt road. One soldier, caught in the blast's epicenter, was hurled several feet into the air before landing in a twisted heap. The wreck burned fiercely, the smoke a black column rising into the overcast sky.

"Good hit," Jack said, his tone devoid of triumph.

"Damn," George muttered, his eyes fixed on the smoldering remains. "That's one hell of a way to go."

"They made their choice," Mike replied flatly, already scanning for new targets.

The radio crackled to life with the voice of Lieutenant Parker. "All units, bridgehead is secure. Hold position and await further orders."

Jack acknowledged the command, then turned to his crew. "Wheels, park us near that ridge. We'll set up there until we get the all-clear."

Tom guided the Sherman to a vantage point overlooking the bridgehead. The tank's engine groaned as it climbed the slight incline, finally coming to a halt behind a patch of rubble that offered some cover.

The battlefield grew quiet as the sounds of gunfire and explosions faded into the distance. The Iron Wolf's crew relaxed slightly, though the tension of the day still hung over them like a storm cloud.

Joe leaned back against the ammo rack, his hands still covered in soot from the shells. "They're not gonna forget this crossing anytime soon," he said.

"They'll come back," Jack replied. "The Germans don't give up ground easily. This was just the first round."

George lit a cigarette, shaking his head. "Let 'em try. As long as we've got Boomers and solid shot, we'll send 'em packing every time."

Jack didn't share George's confidence, but he didn't voice his doubts. The crew had done their job, securing the bridgehead and ensuring the advance could continue. For now, that was enough.

The Iron Wolf sat in its position, its battered hull a testament to the day's chaos. The crew knew the fight wasn't over, but they took solace in the small victory they'd earned.

The battlefield had grown eerily silent as the last rays of sunlight faded, leaving the riverbank shrouded in darkness. The distant crack of sporadic gunfire had ceased, replaced by the occasional groan of the wounded and the muffled hum of engines repositioning in the distance. The Iron Wolf sat idle on the ridge overlooking the Seine, its engine finally silent after a grueling day of combat.

Inside the tank, the crew moved slowly, their exhaustion evident in every motion. The adrenaline that had kept them sharp and alive was gone, leaving behind the weight of fatigue and the memories of what they'd seen.

Joe "Quick Hands" Martinez leaned back against the ammo rack, his helmet tipped over his eyes. "I don't care if I sleep on shells," he muttered, his voice slurred with exhaustion. "I'm out."

George "Grizzly" Thompson was already sprawled across his seat near the bow gun, his cigarette still smoldering in his fingers. "Wake me if the Krauts decide they want another go at us," he said, his tone half-joking, half-resigned.

Mike "Deadeye" Walker rubbed his temples, leaning against the turret wall. "I can still hear that damn machine gun. Every time I close my eyes, it's there. Like it's in my head."

Jack "Boss" Harris sat on the edge of the turret hatch, his eyes fixed on the horizon. The faint glow of burning wreckage on the far bank illuminated the water, casting an orange hue over the river. He didn't reply to his crew's comments; his mind was elsewhere.

Tom "Wheels" Anderson looked up from the driver's seat, his voice soft. "You alright, Boss?"

Jack didn't answer immediately. He reached into his jacket pocket, pulling out the map he'd folded earlier in the day. It was useless now, the positions and plans it outlined already consumed by the chaos of battle. He crumpled it and let it drop to the floor of the tank.

"I'm fine," he said finally, though his voice lacked conviction.

The rest of the crew let it go, too tired to press him further. One by one, they settled into whatever positions they could manage, using jackets, helmets, or even spent shell casings as makeshift pillows.

The cramped confines of the Sherman grew quiet, the steady breathing of his crew a stark contrast to the day's relentless noise. Jack stayed awake, staring out into the darkened battlefield. His thoughts drifted to the bodies in the river, the men torn apart by artillery fire, and the haunting screams of those caught in the collapse of the bridge.

This was success, he thought bitterly. They'd crossed the river, secured the bridgehead, and paved the way for the advance. But at what cost? How many lives had been lost just to move a few miles forward?

He knew the answers didn't matter—not now, not here. All that mattered was surviving the next day, and the day after that, until this war was over. He glanced down at his crew, their faces softened by sleep, and felt a pang of guilt. He was their leader, their anchor, but tonight he felt more like a fraud than a captain.

"Just one more day," Jack whispered to himself, his voice barely audible. "We'll get through one more day."

He slid back into the turret, his head resting against the cold steel wall. Outside, the night deepened, the battlefield settling into an uneasy stillness. Inside the Iron Wolf, the crew drifted into restless sleep, their minds filled with smoke, fire, and the haunting echoes of the day's battle.

Chapter 4: Racing to Belgium

The Iron Wolf roared down the dirt road, its engine humming steadily as it led the column of Shermans toward the Belgian border. The countryside blurred past in shades of green and brown, punctuated by occasional craters and the smoldering remnants of German vehicles. The roads were mostly clear, save for abandoned carts and debris hastily pushed aside by advancing Allied forces.

For the first time in weeks, the crew felt a rare sense of calm. The tension of battle had lifted, replaced by the steady rhythm of the tank's engine and the crunch of its tracks on the gravel.

"Feels weird, doesn't it?" George "Grizzly" Thompson said, leaning back in the bow gun seat. "Rolling through without someone trying to blow us to hell."

"Enjoy it while it lasts," Jack "Boss" Harris replied from the turret. His tone was relaxed, but his eyes stayed on the horizon, scanning for any sign of trouble.

"Hey, I'll take weird over dead any day," George quipped.

Joe "Quick Hands" Martinez chuckled, sitting cross-legged near the ammo rack. He had a rag in hand, polishing a shell casing out of habit. "Weird's good. Means I get to sit back and think about home instead of counting Krauts."

Mike "Deadeye" Walker glanced up from the gunner's seat, his voice laced with skepticism. "Don't get too comfortable. Quiet usually means they're setting something up."

"Deadeye's right," Tom "Wheels" Anderson chimed in from the driver's seat. "This road's too smooth. If I were them, I'd be setting up an ambush just ahead."

Jack nodded, his grip tightening on the turret ring. "We've seen it before. A few miles of peace, and then all hell breaks loose. Stay sharp."

The tank continued its steady advance, the crew settling into a rhythm. The air smelled faintly of diesel and summer grass, a strange combination that reminded Jack of the countryside back home. For a moment, the horrors of war felt distant, as though they belonged to another world.

They passed through a small, abandoned village, its streets empty save for a few stray chickens and a bicycle tipped over near a well. The buildings, though intact, bore the scars of war—shattered windows, bullet-riddled walls, and craters in the cobblestone streets.

"Looks like they left in a hurry," Joe observed, peering out through the side hatch.

"Can you blame 'em?" George replied. "If I saw a bunch of Shermans rolling through, I'd run too."

The column pressed on, the tanks spreading out slightly as the road widened. The radio crackled to life with a message from Lieutenant Parker. "All units, keep moving. Scattered resistance reported ahead, but no major enemy forces. Stay alert."

"Scattered resistance," Mike muttered. "That's just code for 'you're gonna run into trouble.'"

Jack smirked but didn't disagree. "Better to expect it and not get it than the other way around."

As if on cue, a distant crack shattered the calm. The sharp report of a rifle echoed through the air, followed by the distinctive chatter of an MG42.

"Contact!" Jack shouted, snapping back into combat mode. "Grizzly, get on that bow gun! Deadeye, scan for the source of that fire!"

"I see it!" Mike called, his hands already spinning the turret. "Machine-gun nest, two o'clock, tucked behind those sandbags!"

Jack swung the periscope toward the position. The Germans had set up a small ambush, with a machine gun covering the road and riflemen positioned along a nearby hedge. The first few infantrymen from the column had already hit the dirt, scrambling for cover.

"Quick Hands, load up a Boomer!" Jack ordered.

"Boomer loaded!" Joe shouted, slamming the round into the breech.

"Deadeye, take out that nest!" Jack barked.

Mike fired, the 75mm high-explosive round streaking toward the target. The shell detonated on impact, sending sandbags, dirt, and bodies flying. The machine gun went silent, its crew obliterated in the blast.

"Target down!" Mike called.

"Nice shot!" George added, firing the bow gun at the retreating riflemen. The .30-caliber rounds tore through the underbrush, cutting down several soldiers as they tried to flee.

"Wheels, keep us moving!" Jack commanded. "We're sitting ducks if we stay here."

Tom revved the engine, the Iron Wolf surging forward. The other Shermans followed, their guns firing sporadically at the retreating Germans. A few stray rifle shots pinged harmlessly off the tank's armor, but the ambush had been broken.

As the tank crested a small hill, the road ahead opened up into a wide, flat expanse of farmland. Smoke from the destroyed machine-gun nest drifted lazily behind them, fading into the afternoon sky.

"Well, so much for quiet," George muttered, lighting a cigarette with shaky hands.

"We're still alive," Jack said, his tone even. "That's all that matters. Quick Hands, reload. Deadeye, keep an eye on that tree line. We've got miles to go before we're clear."

The Iron Wolf rolled on, its crew shaken but intact. The open road had reminded them, however briefly, of a world outside the war. But the sudden skirmish was a harsh reminder that danger was never far behind.

The open farmland stretched out in every direction, rows of golden wheat swaying in the wind. The dirt road snaked through the fields, bordered by dense tree lines that offered perfect cover for an ambush. The Iron Wolf led the column, its engine rumbling steadily as the crew remained on high alert.

"Anything?" Jack asked, his voice tense as he scanned the tree line through his periscope.

"Nothing yet, Boss," Mike replied, his eyes glued to the gun sight. "But this setup screams 'ambush.' I don't like it."

"Wheels, keep us slow and steady," Jack said. "Grizzly, stay ready on that bow gun. If anything moves, take it out."

The radio crackled with a warning from Lieutenant Parker. "All units, we've got reports of enemy armor in the area. Panzer IVs and infantry with anti-tank weapons. Stay tight and watch your flanks."

Jack cursed under his breath. The Panzer IV was no Tiger, but its 75mm gun was more than capable of punching through a Sherman's armor. Combined with infantry wielding Panzerfausts, the situation was a powder keg waiting to explode.

"Deadeye, what's our loadout?" Jack asked.

"Solid shot loaded," Mike replied. "Boomers on standby. Quick Hands is keeping us stacked."

"Good," Jack said. "We'll need to hit hard if they come at us."

The column pressed forward, the tension mounting with every passing second. The wheat fields swayed innocently in the breeze, but the crew knew better. They were walking into a trap.

And then it happened.

The first shot came from the right, a muzzle flash from the tree line followed by the thunderous roar of a Panzer IV's cannon. The round slammed into the lead Sherman, piercing its side armor and igniting the ammunition. The tank exploded in a fireball, its turret blown skyward before crashing down in a shower of metal and gore.

"Ambush! Right flank!" Jack shouted. "Wheels, hard left! Get us out of their line of fire!"

Tom jerked the controls, the Iron Wolf lurching to the left as another shell screamed past, narrowly missing them. The radio came alive with frantic voices, commanders shouting orders and reporting enemy positions.

"Deadeye, Panzer IV at two o'clock!" Jack barked. "Solid shot, now!"

"On target!" Mike shouted, spinning the turret and firing. The 75mm round streaked across the field, slamming into the Panzer's side. The German tank shuddered, its armor buckling under the impact, before erupting into flames.

"Target down!" Mike called.

"Quick Hands, load another solid shot!" Jack ordered.

"Loaded!" Joe replied, his hands moving with practiced speed.

The Germans weren't done. Infantry poured out of the tree line, Panzerfausts slung over their shoulders as they charged toward the Shermans. One soldier fired, the rocket-propelled grenade striking the second Sherman in the column. The explosion ripped through the tank's engine compartment, and moments later, its turret exploded outward, sending shards of metal and a gruesome spray of blood and body parts into the air.

"Jesus Christ," George muttered, his voice shaking. "They're cutting us apart."

"Grizzly, mow down that infantry!" Jack ordered.

George opened up with the bow gun, the .30 caliber rounds tearing into the charging Germans. Several soldiers dropped, their bodies jerking as the bullets found their mark, but more kept coming.

"Deadeye, another Panzer IV at three o'clock!" Jack shouted.

"Got it!" Mike replied, swinging the turret toward the new target. The German tank was advancing through the wheat, its gun already trained on the Shermans. Mike fired, the solid shot striking the Panzer's front plate. The armor held, but the impact disabled its gun, forcing the crew to retreat.

"Hit it again!" Jack ordered.

Mike fired a second time, this round punching through the Panzer's hull. Flames erupted from the tank as its crew bailed out, only to be cut down by Allied machine-gun fire.

"Two Panzers down," Jack said, his voice steady despite the chaos. "Quick Hands, switch to Boomers. Grizzly, keep that bow gun hot. Wheels, move us forward and out of this kill zone."

The Iron Wolf pressed ahead, its tracks grinding over the torn-up road. The remaining German infantry scattered, some retreating back into the tree line while others were cut down by suppressing fire from the Shermans and advancing infantry.

The ambush had been brutal, but the column was moving again. Jack took a deep breath, forcing himself to focus. They'd survived another trap, but the cost was clear in the burning wrecks of the Shermans left behind.

"Deadeye, keep scanning," Jack said. "They're not done yet."

The Iron Wolf rolled on, its crew battered but alive, ready for whatever came next.

The Iron Wolf rumbled into a shallow depression flanked by scattered trees and low stone walls. The ambush had scattered the column, and now the Shermans were regrouping under sporadic German fire. Infantry streamed through the brush, their shapes flickering like ghosts between the trees, too close for comfort.

"Boss, they're coming right at us!" George "Grizzly" Thompson shouted, gripping the bow gun controls. "This isn't an ambush anymore; it's a damn charge!"

Jack "Boss" Harris swung his periscope toward the advancing Germans. Dozens of them were rushing through the underbrush, some with rifles, others carrying grenades or Panzerfausts. They were too close for the cannon.

"Grizzly, it's all you," Jack barked. "Wheels, keep us steady. Quick Hands, be ready to reload if we need the turret for anything heavy."

George gritted his teeth, his hands steady despite the chaos. "Got it, Boss. They wanna get up close? Fine by me."

As the first wave of Germans broke into the open, George opened fire with the bow-mounted .30 caliber machine gun. The gun spat a steady stream of bullets, the muzzle flashes lighting up the gloom beneath the trees.

The first row of attackers fell instantly, their bodies jerking as the rounds tore into them. Blood sprayed across the ground, and screams rang out as the charging soldiers collapsed into crumpled heaps.

More Germans surged forward, firing wildly as they advanced. Bullets pinged off the Iron Wolf's hull, some ricocheting harmlessly, others embedding themselves in the thick steel.

"They're all over us!" Tom "Wheels" Anderson shouted from the driver's seat, gripping the controls tightly.

"Stay calm!" Jack commanded. "Grizzly's got this. Keep us moving slow, just enough to keep the infantry from swarming us."

George's aim didn't waver as he mowed down another wave of attackers. A soldier armed with a Panzerfaust darted out from behind a tree, raising the weapon to fire.

"Panzerfaust! Ten o'clock!" Mike "Deadeye" Walker called out.

"I see him!" George shouted, swiveling the bow gun toward the target. He fired a burst, the rounds striking the soldier squarely in the chest. The man staggered backward, the Panzerfaust slipping from his hands before he collapsed in a pool of blood.

The chaos intensified as the Germans attempted to flank the Sherman. A group of three infantrymen sprinted toward the tank, rifles at the ready. George swung the bow gun, cutting them down before they could reach cover. One man screamed as a round tore through his abdomen, his intestines spilling out as he fell to the ground.

"Reloading!" George shouted, his voice hoarse from yelling. He fumbled with a fresh belt of ammunition, his hands shaking as he worked quickly to feed it into the gun.

"Keep it together, Grizzly!" Jack said. "Quick Hands, get on the loader's hatch and cover him if they get too close."

Joe "Quick Hands" Martinez grabbed his M1 carbine and climbed halfway out of the loader's hatch, his eyes scanning for any soldiers who might have slipped past George's fire. He spotted one crawling toward the tank, a grenade clutched in his hand.

"Grenade, left side!" Joe yelled, firing three quick shots. The soldier slumped forward, the grenade rolling harmlessly from his grip.

"Nice one, Quick Hands," Jack said. "Grizzly, how's that bow gun?"

"Locked and loaded!" George replied, slamming the ammunition belt into place. "Let's finish this."

The remaining Germans hesitated, the relentless fire from the Iron Wolf cutting down their numbers with brutal efficiency. Another burst from George's gun sprayed the tree line, the rounds ripping through branches and into the soldiers hiding behind them. Blood splattered the bark, and several men fell, their bodies twitching as the bullets found their marks.

Finally, the attack faltered. The surviving Germans began to retreat, dragging the wounded with them. Some dropped their weapons entirely, disappearing into the underbrush as fast as their legs could carry them.

"Deadeye, watch the retreat," Jack said. "If they regroup, I want to know about it."

Mike scanned the horizon through the turret, his hands steady on the controls. "They're gone, Boss. We scared 'em off."

Jack exhaled deeply, the tension slowly releasing from his shoulders. "Good work, everyone. Grizzly, you just saved our hides."

George leaned back in his seat, sweat pouring down his face. "Just another day in paradise, Boss." His voice was tired but tinged with pride.

The Iron Wolf rumbled forward again, leaving the bloody field behind. The ground was littered with bodies, some twisted and broken, others eerily still. The crew didn't dwell on it. There was no time to reflect—they still had a mission to complete, and Belgium wasn't going to wait.

"Let's keep rolling," Jack said. "We've got more work to do."

The small town ahead was eerily quiet, its cobblestone streets empty save for the occasional stray dog or overturned cart. The Allied infantry moved cautiously, darting between the cover of ruined buildings as they prepared to clear the area. Jack "Boss" Harris sat in the Iron Wolf's turret, scanning the crumbling rooftops for any sign of movement.

"Keep your eyes sharp," Jack said, his voice tense. "We've got reports of snipers and machine-gun nests. Wheels, hold position until the infantry's ready."

"Got it, Boss," Tom "Wheels" Anderson replied, his hands steady on the controls.

The radio crackled with an order from Lieutenant Parker. "Iron Wolf, you're up. Lead the charge into the town and provide covering fire for the infantry. Expect resistance in the central square. Keep moving and stay coordinated."

Jack acknowledged the order, his voice calm despite the weight of the task. "Deadeye, load up a Boomer. Quick Hands, keep the shells coming. Grizzly, you're on watch for infantry—anything that moves, you light it up."

"Boomer loaded!" Joe "Quick Hands" Martinez called out, slamming the high-explosive round into the breech.

The Iron Wolf rolled forward, its engine growling as it led the column into the narrow streets. The buildings on either side were scarred by previous battles, their facades riddled with bullet holes and their windows shattered. The tank's tracks crushed discarded rubble and twisted metal as it advanced.

"Contact! Machine gun, second floor, left side!" Mike "Deadeye" Walker shouted.

Jack swung his periscope toward the building. The flash of a muzzle and the sharp chatter of an MG42 confirmed the threat. Bullets rained down on the infantry behind the tank, forcing them to dive for cover.

"Deadeye, take it out!" Jack ordered.

Mike adjusted the turret, aiming for the upper floor. The Sherman's cannon roared, the high-explosive round slamming into the building. The wall crumbled under the impact, collapsing inward and burying the machine-gun crew in a cloud of dust and debris.

"Target neutralized," Mike reported, his tone steady.

The tank rumbled forward, the infantry following in its wake. Sporadic rifle fire echoed from side streets, but the Germans were disorganized, their resistance faltering under the Sherman's firepower.

As the Iron Wolf approached the town square, the resistance stiffened. German soldiers poured out of alleyways and doorways, some carrying Panzerfausts while others manned makeshift barricades.

"Quick Hands, another Boomer!" Jack shouted.

"Loaded!" Joe replied.

"Deadeye, take out that barricade!"

The cannon fired again, the high-explosive round obliterating the wooden barrier and sending German soldiers flying. The force of the blast flung one man into the air, his body landing lifeless in the middle of the street.

"They're trying to regroup in that building ahead!" George "Grizzly" Thompson called out, pointing toward a three-story structure with Germans pouring into it.

"Deadeye, bring it down," Jack said.

Mike didn't hesitate. The Sherman's gun roared, the shell striking the building near its base. The explosion shook the entire structure, the walls groaning as they began to give way.

Inside, a German soldier screamed, his voice carrying over the din of battle. He scrambled toward the door, but it was too late. The building collapsed, the upper floors caving in and burying him under tons of rubble. The scream was abruptly cut off, replaced by the grinding noise of settling debris.

"Building's down," Mike said grimly, watching the dust settle.

"Grizzly, sweep for any stragglers," Jack ordered.

George opened up with the bow gun, spraying the rubble and nearby alleyways to ensure no Germans were hiding. The infantry surged forward, moving past the tank to secure the square.

"All clear," came the radio report from one of the infantry squad leaders.

Jack took a deep breath, his grip loosening on the turret controls. "Wheels, hold position. Deadeye, keep scanning. Quick Hands, reload. We're not done yet."

The crew worked in tense silence, their eyes fixed on the surrounding streets. The town was secure, but the cost of the battle was etched into the bloodied cobblestones and the rubble-strewn square.

"Another job done," George muttered, lighting a cigarette with shaky hands.

"For now," Jack replied. "Let's hope Belgium's ready for us."

The Iron Wolf stood tall amidst the ruins, its steel hull scarred but unbroken. The battle for the town was over, but the war rolled on, and so did they.

The Iron Wolf sat parked on the edge of the ruined town, its engine quiet for the first time in hours. The battlefield had fallen eerily silent, save for the occasional sound of Allied infantry clearing nearby buildings. Smoke still lingered in the air, mixing with the scent of diesel and scorched earth. The crew had a rare moment of respite and were determined to make the most of it.

"Grizzly, how's that bow gun?" Jack asked, leaning against the turret and sipping from his canteen.

George "Grizzly" Thompson was crouched near the tank's front, his sleeves rolled up as he tinkered with the .30-caliber machine gun. "Jammed during that last push," he muttered, twisting a wrench with practiced ease. "Had to clear it mid-firefight. Damn thing almost got us killed."

"You cleared it just in time," Joe "Quick Hands" Martinez chimed in from his spot near the ammo rack. He was cleaning soot off a spent shell casing, his hands moving automatically. "Don't think I've ever seen you move that fast, Grizz."

George grinned, his grease-streaked face lighting up with mock indignation. "Fast? I was a blur. Like lightning. You probably couldn't see it from back there, Quick Hands."

"Sure, Grizz," Joe replied, rolling his eyes. "You're a regular hero."

The banter drew a laugh from Mike "Deadeye" Walker, who was perched on the turret, cleaning his gun sights. "Only time Grizzly's fast is when there's food on the line."

"You're one to talk, Deadeye," George shot back, gesturing with his wrench. "I've seen you turn into a damn raccoon when there's coffee around."

"Alright, alright," Jack interrupted, chuckling as he leaned against the tank's hull. "Save the insults for the Germans. Grizzly, finish up with that bow gun. Wheels, check the tracks. I don't want any surprises if we've got to move in a hurry."

Tom "Wheels" Anderson gave a thumbs-up from where he was inspecting the treads. "Tracks look good, Boss. A little loose on the left, but nothing serious."

"Fix it anyway," Jack said. "We've got time."

As the crew busied themselves with their tasks, the atmosphere grew lighter. The horrors of the day, the collapsing buildings, and the screams of dying men felt distant, muted by the camaraderie that bound them together.

"Hey, Deadeye," Joe said, grinning as he held up the shell casing he'd been cleaning. "Think this one's got a kill on it? You nailed that barricade like a damn sniper."

Mike smirked, tossing his rag onto the turret. "Every shot I take's a kill, Quick Hands. You just keep feeding me rounds, and I'll keep making magic."

"Magic, huh?" George said, standing up and wiping his hands on his pants. "You missed that Panzer by a mile last week. I had to save your ass with the bow gun."

"Missed?" Mike shot back, feigning outrage. "That was a warning shot. Gave them a chance to surrender."

The crew burst into laughter, the sound echoing across the quiet town square. It was a rare moment of levity, a reminder of the humanity they still clung to despite the brutal reality of war.

Jack allowed himself a smile as he watched his crew. These men were his family now, bound together by steel, sweat, and survival. He climbed up onto the turret, letting the warmth of the fading sun settle on his shoulders.

"We'll be rolling again soon," Jack said, his voice cutting through the laughter. "Enjoy this while it lasts. Tomorrow, we're back in the thick of it."

The crew nodded, their laughter fading but their spirits lifted. Grizzly gave the bow gun one final test, the weapon's mechanisms clicking smoothly. "All set, Boss. She's good as new."

"Good," Jack said, patting the tank's turret. "The Iron Wolf's ready to hunt again."

As the sun dipped below the horizon, the crew settled back into their routine, preparing for whatever lay ahead. For now, they had their tank, their camaraderie, and the rare gift of a few peaceful moments. It wasn't much, but it was enough.

Chapter 5: Entering Belgium

The Iron Wolf crossed into Belgium under a gray, overcast sky. The air was thick with the promise of rain, and the narrow roads were slick with mud from recent storms. The crew felt the shift immediately—the tension, the quiet resolve of soldiers preparing for a fight. The Germans here weren't retreating anymore. They were dug in, fighting with the ferocity of men with nothing left to lose.

"Boss, I don't like this," George "Grizzly" Thompson said, his voice tight as he manned the bow gun. "They've been hitting us hard for days, and now it's too quiet again. Never a good sign."

"Agreed," Jack "Boss" Harris replied from the turret. His eyes scanned the horizon through his periscope, searching for anything out of place. "Keep your eyes sharp. Deadeye, how's our loadout?"

"Solid shot loaded. Boomers and Willie Pete standing by," Mike "Deadeye" Walker replied from the gunner's seat.

"Good. Quick Hands, keep us stocked," Jack said.

Joe "Quick Hands" Martinez gave a quick thumbs-up as he checked the ammo racks. "Locked and loaded, Boss. Ready for whatever they throw at us."

The radio crackled with a transmission from Lieutenant Parker. "All units, we've got reports of heavy resistance ahead. German positions are fortified along the ridge, likely with anti-tank emplacements and infantry support. Proceed with caution and coordinate fire."

Jack acknowledged the order and turned to his crew. "Alright, you heard him. Wheels, keep us moving slow and steady. Grizzly, stay on that bow gun—if anything moves, I want it gone. Deadeye, be ready to hit any bunkers or guns we spot."

As the Iron Wolf crept forward, the terrain became more challenging. The narrow road wound through a dense forest, the tree line pressing close on either side. The column moved cautiously, the Shermans spaced out to avoid presenting an easy target.

The first shot came without warning.

An explosion tore through the trees ahead, sending dirt and debris raining down. The lead Sherman shuddered to a halt, its hull blackened by the impact of a German Pak 40 anti-tank gun.

"Contact! Dug-in positions on the ridge!" Jack shouted. "Wheels, get us some cover! Deadeye, find that gun!"

Tom "Wheels" Anderson jerked the tank to the side, maneuvering the Iron Wolf into a shallow ditch. Another shell screamed past, striking the road behind them and gouging out a massive crater.

"Got it!" Mike shouted, his voice sharp with focus. "Pak 40 at one o'clock, behind sandbags."

"Boomer, now!" Jack ordered.

"Boomer loaded!" Joe called.

Mike fired, the 75mm high-explosive round slamming into the gun position. The blast obliterated the sandbags, sending shrapnel and dirt flying. The gun crew was thrown backward, their bodies crumpling like rag dolls.

"Target down!" Mike reported.

Before they could celebrate, a burst of machine-gun fire erupted from the tree line, raking the infantry advancing alongside the tanks. Men dove for cover, but a few went down hard, their cries of pain cutting through the chaos.

"Grizzly, take out that machine gun!" Jack ordered.

George swung the bow gun toward the treeline, firing a sustained burst. The .30-caliber rounds tore through the foliage, silencing the MG42 and sending its crew scrambling.

"Nice work, Grizz," Jack said. "Deadeye, scan for more targets. Quick Hands, load another Boomer. Wheels, keep us moving."

The Iron Wolf pushed forward, its tracks grinding over the muddy road. The Germans weren't finished yet. Another Pak 40 fired from a position further up the ridge, the shell striking the Sherman behind them. The tank's side armor buckled, and flames began pouring from its hatches.

"Damn it," Jack muttered, swinging his periscope toward the ridge. "Deadeye, take out that second gun!"

"On it!" Mike replied, firing another high-explosive round. The shell struck the Pak 40 dead-on, the explosion engulfing the gun and its crew in a fiery blast.

"All clear," Mike said, his voice taut with adrenaline.

Jack keyed the radio. "Iron Wolf to command, two anti-tank positions neutralized. Infantry advancing. We're holding for now."

The radio crackled back with Lieutenant Parker's voice. "Good work, Iron Wolf. Keep pushing forward. We need that ridge secured."

Jack turned to his crew, his voice steady but firm. "We're not done yet. Reload, regroup, and get ready for the next fight. These bastards aren't going down easy."

The Iron Wolf pressed on, its crew battle-hardened and determined. The enemy was fierce, but they were ready for whatever came next.

The Iron Wolf crept up the muddy road as the rest of the tank company spread out into a staggered formation. The woods on either side of the road were dense, but the ridge above was the real concern. It loomed ominously in the distance, the perfect vantage point for enemy artillery.

"Boss, I don't like this," Tom "Wheels" Anderson muttered, gripping the controls. "Feels like we're walking into the lion's den."

Jack "Boss" Harris scanned the horizon through his periscope. The sky had darkened, and the air was thick with the metallic scent of rain and smoke. "Stay sharp. Grizzly, keep an eye on the flanks. Deadeye, be ready to target anything that fires from that ridge."

The radio crackled with a warning from Lieutenant Parker. "All units, be advised. German artillery positions have been reported in the area. Likely Nebelwerfers. Keep your formation loose and stay mobile."

"Nebelwerfers," Mike "Deadeye" Walker muttered, shaking his head. "Great. Nothing like a little 'Screaming Meemies' to ruin your day."

"Better than sitting still," Joe "Quick Hands" Martinez added as he adjusted the ammo rack. "If they hit us, we're toast."

The advance continued cautiously, the tanks inching forward as the infantry cleared the surrounding woods. The tension was palpable, every creak of a tree branch or distant echo putting the crew on edge.

Then the first barrage came.

A piercing, bone-chilling wail ripped through the air, followed by the thunderous explosion of rockets slamming into the earth. The Nebelwerfers had opened fire, their distinct howl earning them their sinister nickname.

"Get us out of here, Wheels!" Jack shouted, gripping the turret controls.

Tom slammed the tank into reverse, maneuvering toward a shallow depression for cover. Rockets screamed overhead, slamming into the road and surrounding terrain. Dirt, metal, and body parts were flung into the air as the barrage tore through the Allied formation.

"Jesus!" George "Grizzly" Thompson yelled as a shell exploded nearby, rattling the Iron Wolf. "They're zeroing in on us!"

Through the periscope, Jack saw a Sherman in the column take a direct hit. The rocket struck its engine compartment, and the tank erupted into a fireball, its turret flying into the air before crashing down in a twisted heap. Flames consumed the hull, and the crew's screams were drowned out by the roar of the inferno.

"They're gone," Mike muttered, his voice tight with anger and fear. "Whole damn crew…"

"Focus!" Jack barked, forcing himself to stay calm. "Deadeye, can you see the launchers?"

Mike swung the turret toward the ridge, scanning through the smoke and chaos. "I've got movement! Looks like the launchers are just behind that tree line, two o'clock!"

"Quick Hands, load up a Boomer," Jack ordered. "Grizzly, keep that bow gun ready in case infantry shows up."

"Boomer loaded!" Joe called, slamming the shell into the breech.

"Wheels, get us a firing position!" Jack said.

Tom pushed the Iron Wolf forward, using the uneven terrain as cover. Another barrage of rockets screamed overhead, one landing so close that the tank rocked violently, dirt raining down on the hull.

"Hold us here!" Jack shouted. "Deadeye, take the shot!"

Mike lined up the turret, his hands steady despite the chaos. "On target… firing!"

The Sherman's 75mm cannon roared, the high-explosive round streaking toward the ridge. The shell struck one of the Nebelwerfer launchers, the explosion igniting the rockets still loaded in the frame. The resulting chain reaction obliterated the launcher and its crew, sending flames and shrapnel into the air.

"Target destroyed!" Mike called out.

"Good hit!" Jack replied. "Quick Hands, reload!"

"Boomer reloaded!" Joe shouted.

"Deadeye, find the next launcher!" Jack ordered.

"I've got it!" Mike said, swinging the turret toward a second position. He fired again, the shell slamming into another Nebelwerfer. The launcher disintegrated, its crew vaporized in the blast.

The rocket fire began to slow as the German positions were systematically taken out. The remaining Shermans joined the assault, their cannons roaring as they targeted the ridge. The barrage of "Screaming Meemies" gave way to silence, broken only by the crackling of fires and the groans of the wounded.

"All units, the ridge is clear," Lieutenant Parker's voice crackled over the radio. "Regroup and prepare to advance."

Jack exhaled deeply, his hands trembling slightly as he adjusted his helmet. "Good work, everyone. Grizzly, keep scanning. Wheels, get us back in line. Quick Hands, make sure we're stocked."

The crew moved efficiently, their exhaustion visible but their resolve unbroken. The Iron Wolf had survived another encounter, but the cost was evident in the smoldering wreckage of the destroyed Sherman and the lives lost to the German artillery.

As the tank rolled forward, Jack allowed himself a brief moment to reflect. The Germans were fighting harder now, their desperation making them more dangerous. But no matter the odds, the Iron Wolf and its crew would press on. They had no other choice.

The Iron Wolf sat at the edge of a muddy field, its engine rumbling as Allied infantry prepared for an assault on the German defensive line ahead. Through his periscope, Jack "Boss" Harris could see the enemy fortifications—a series of trenches and bunkers reinforced with sandbags and barbed wire. German soldiers moved purposefully within the defenses, setting up machine guns and preparing for the coming attack.

Jack keyed the radio. "All units, this is Iron Wolf. Infantry's gearing up for the push. We're laying down smoke and suppressing fire to cover their advance. Deadeye, Quick Hands—get ready to work."

"Willie Pete loaded," Joe "Quick Hands" Martinez called out, pulling a white phosphorus shell from the rack and slamming it into the breech.

Mike "Deadeye" Walker adjusted the turret, his voice steady. "Ready to fire, Boss. Just say the word."

Jack took a deep breath, scanning the enemy positions one last time. "Wheels, move us up slow. Deadeye, lay smoke on those trenches. Grizzly, keep your bow gun sweeping for any infantry trying to flank us."

"Got it, Boss," George "Grizzly" Thompson replied, his hands gripping the bow gun controls.

Tom "Wheels" Anderson eased the Sherman forward, its tracks grinding through the mud. The tank moved deliberately, its bulk providing cover for the infantry advancing behind it. Jack's voice rang out over the intercom.

"Deadeye, fire!"

The Iron Wolf's cannon roared, the white phosphorus round streaking across the field. It exploded in a blinding burst over the German trenches, thick clouds of white smoke billowing out and obscuring the defenders' line of sight.

"First round out," Mike reported. "They can't see a damn thing now."

"Quick Hands, reload another Willie Pete," Jack ordered.

"Already on it!" Joe replied, slamming another shell into the breech.

"Grizzly, anything moving out there?" Jack asked.

"Not yet," George replied, scanning the smoke. "But they'll start blind-firing any second."

The infantry surged forward, their boots pounding the muddy field as they moved under the cover of the Sherman's firepower. Machine-gun fire erupted from the German line, but the thick smoke from the phosphorus rounds threw their aim off, the bullets pinging harmlessly into the dirt and ricocheting off the tank's armor.

"Deadeye, target those bunkers with Boomers," Jack ordered. "Take them out before the infantry gets pinned."

"On it," Mike replied, switching rounds and taking aim. "Boomer loaded… firing!"

The 75mm high-explosive shell slammed into a sandbagged bunker, detonating with a deafening explosion. The blast sent chunks of concrete and sandbags flying, and the German machine gun inside went silent.

"Bunker's down," Mike called.

"Good hit," Jack said. "Keep it up. Quick Hands, keep those Boomers coming."

The German defenders began to recover, firing blindly through the smoke and launching flares to try and regain visibility. A burst of machine-gun fire tore into the advancing infantry, and several men went down in a spray of blood and screams.

"Grizzly, hit that MG nest!" Jack barked.

George swung the bow gun toward the source of the fire, opening up with the .30 caliber. The rounds chewed through the sandbags and struck the machine-gun crew, cutting them down. One soldier clutched his chest as he fell backward, disappearing into the trench.

"They're down!" George shouted.

The Iron Wolf pressed forward, its cannon roaring as it cleared one position after another. Each blast of white phosphorus and high-explosive rounds gave the infantry the cover and momentum they needed to reach the trenches.

Jack keyed the radio. "Infantry is at the line! Keep suppressing and watch for counterattacks!"

A German soldier emerged from the smoke, a Panzerfaust clutched in his hands. Before he could fire, Joe popped out of the loader's hatch with his carbine, firing two quick shots. The soldier went down, the rocket launcher slipping from his grasp.

"Nice shooting, Quick Hands," Jack said.

"Someone's gotta watch our backs," Joe replied, sliding back into the tank.

As the last of the German defenders were overwhelmed, the trench line fell silent. The infantry moved methodically through the positions, clearing out stragglers and securing the area. The Iron Wolf rumbled to a halt near the edge of the trenches, its crew scanning for any remaining threats.

"All units, the line is secure," came the voice of Lieutenant Parker over the radio. "Good work. Regroup and prepare to push forward."

Jack exhaled, the tension easing slightly. "Good job, everyone. Wheels, hold us here. Deadeye, reload. Grizzly, keep your eyes on the flanks. This isn't over yet."

The Iron Wolf stood as a steel sentinel over the captured line, its crew battered but victorious. For now, the way forward was clear, but Jack knew the enemy wouldn't make the next mile any easier.

The Iron Wolf sat at the edge of the captured trench line, its engine idling softly as the crew scanned the battlefield. The smoke from the phosphorus rounds still hung in the air, mingling with the acrid stench of burnt metal, scorched earth, and blood. The once-pristine field was now a graveyard, littered with bodies, shattered equipment, and the smoldering remnants of bunkers and machine-gun nests.

Inside the tank, the mood was subdued. The adrenaline from the assault had begun to wear off, replaced by the weight of what they had just done.

"Jesus," George "Grizzly" Thompson muttered from his bow gun position, staring at the devastation. "We tore this place apart."

"Had to," Jack "Boss" Harris replied from the turret. His voice was steady, but his eyes lingered on the battlefield. "If we didn't, it'd be us lying out there."

"Still," Joe "Quick Hands" Martinez said quietly, leaning back against the ammo rack. "Look at them. Most of those guys were probably just kids, same as us."

Through his periscope, Jack saw what Joe meant. A few German soldiers had been caught in the phosphorus blast, their bodies blackened and twisted by the searing heat. One man lay clutching his rifle, his face frozen in a grimace of terror and pain. Another had been caught mid-run, his legs gone and the earth around him soaked with blood.

"Doesn't matter how old they are," Mike "Deadeye" Walker said from his gunner's seat, his tone sharper than usual. "They were trying to kill us. If we didn't hit them first, we'd be the ones lying out there, burned to a crisp or worse."

Joe nodded, but his expression didn't change. "Yeah. But knowing that doesn't make it easier."

"Grizzly," Jack said, interrupting the silence. "What do you see on the flanks?"

"Clear so far," George replied, though his voice was distant. His usual bravado was gone, replaced by a grim resignation. "No movement. Just… bodies."

Jack exhaled, leaning back in his seat. "War isn't supposed to be easy. You think about it too much, it'll eat you alive. Focus on the job. Keep each other alive. That's all that matters."

The crew nodded, each man processing the destruction in his own way. Through the turret hatch, Jack could see the infantry moving among the wreckage, their expressions grim as they cleared out the trenches. One soldier paused to check on a wounded German, but it was clear there was nothing he could do. The man's blood soaked into the dirt, joining countless others who had fallen on the same ground.

Tom "Wheels" Anderson broke the silence. "You think they feel the same way about us? The Germans, I mean. When they see us coming, do they hate us? Fear us?"

"Probably both," Jack replied. "Same way we feel when we see them. But fear doesn't stop the shells from flying. It's just the way it is."

"Doesn't make it right," Joe said softly.

"No," Jack agreed. "But that's not our call to make. We do the job, or we don't make it home."

The tank fell quiet again, the weight of Jack's words settling over the crew. Outside, the battlefield was still, the only movement the faint flicker of flames licking at the remains of a destroyed bunker. The Iron Wolf had done its job—laid down fire, crushed defenses, and cleared the way—but the toll of their firepower was impossible to ignore.

"Boss," Mike said after a moment. "We've still got a long way to go, don't we?"

Jack glanced at him, his face hard but understanding. "Yeah. We do."

The crew returned to their tasks, checking the ammunition, clearing debris from the treads, and keeping their minds busy. The battlefield was behind them now, but its echoes would linger in their thoughts long after the tank moved on.

The Iron Wolf stood silent, a monument to both the power and the cost of war.

The first breath of winter swept through the countryside as the Iron Wolf parked in a makeshift bivouac near the edge of a dense forest. The trees, stripped of their leaves, stood like skeletal sentinels against the pale gray sky. A biting wind carried with it the promise of harsher days ahead, cutting through even the thickest jackets and seeping into the steel confines of the Sherman.

"Feels like we've walked into an icebox," George "Grizzly" Thompson muttered, rubbing his gloved hands together as he leaned against the bow gun. His breath came out in frosty puffs. "And it's only gonna get worse."

"Quit complaining," Mike "Deadeye" Walker replied from his spot near the turret. "Cold means the mud'll freeze. Easier to move the tank."

"Yeah?" George shot back. "Tell that to my frozen fingers."

The crew had taken a rare break to stretch outside the tank, each man trying to shake off the tension of the last engagement. The mood was subdued, the recent carnage fresh in their minds. Around them, other crews and infantry huddled together, their faces grim as they prepared for the next phase of the campaign.

Tom "Wheels" Anderson sat near the Iron Wolf's tracks, adjusting his boots and pulling his jacket tighter. "You'd think command could get us better gear. My toes are damn near frostbitten already."

"They're saving the good stuff for the brass," Joe "Quick Hands" Martinez said with a grin, his teeth chattering as he spoke. "We get the leftovers."

Jack "Boss" Harris stood on the turret, his eyes scanning the treeline. The overcast sky and the swirling wind created a sense of unease. The cold wasn't just a physical enemy—it was psychological, draining energy and morale with every passing hour.

"Gear or no gear, we've got to keep moving," Jack said, his voice carrying over the wind. "This weather's only going to slow us down more if we let it."

"Slow us down?" George scoffed. "This weather's trying to kill us as much as the Krauts are."

"Then don't let it," Jack replied sharply, his gaze snapping to George. "You've survived worse. We all have."

The crew fell silent, Jack's words a reminder of the resilience that had brought them this far. The Iron Wolf wasn't just a tank—it was their lifeline, their shield against the chaos of the war. Inside it, they were a team; outside, they were exposed to the merciless elements.

As they climbed back into the Sherman, the crew settled into their familiar positions. The steel walls of the tank offered little insulation, but the warmth of the engine provided a welcome reprieve from the freezing wind.

Jack keyed the radio, listening for updates. Lieutenant Parker's voice came through, strained but resolute. "All units, prepare for movement at first light. Weather's turning, and the Germans know it. Expect resistance as we push deeper into the Ardennes."

"Copy that, Lieutenant," Jack replied. He turned to his crew. "You heard him. Rest up while you can. Tomorrow's going to be rough."

The men nodded, each retreating into their own thoughts. George lit a cigarette, the faint glow illuminating his face in the dim interior. Joe leaned back against the ammo rack, closing his eyes as he tried to block out the cold. Mike adjusted his sights, ensuring the gun was ready for whatever came next, while Tom adjusted the controls, his hands moving instinctively over the dials.

Jack leaned against the turret ring, his breath misting in the frigid air. The wind howled outside, rattling the trees and creating an eerie symphony that set his nerves on edge. The campaign in Belgium was far from over, and with winter closing in, the stakes were higher than ever.

The Iron Wolf sat like a silent guardian in the cold, its crew huddled inside, preparing for the battles yet to come.

Chapter 6: Into the Hurtgen Forest

The Iron Wolf crept into the dense maze of the Hurtgen Forest, its tracks grinding against the mud-slicked ground. Towering trees loomed on all sides, their skeletal branches forming a canopy that blocked out most of the sunlight. The terrain was suffocating, every inch of it designed to swallow men and machines alike. The Germans called it the *Grünes Inferno*—Green Hell—and it was easy to see why.

"Boss, this place gives me the creeps," George "Grizzly" Thompson muttered, his eyes darting between the trees as he manned the bow gun. "Feels like the trees are watching us."

"They're not the problem," Jack "Boss" Harris replied from the turret, scanning the narrow path ahead through his periscope. "It's what's hiding behind them that'll kill us. Stay sharp."

"Can't see five feet in this mess," Mike "Deadeye" Walker said from the gunner's seat, frustration edging his voice. "If they've got AT guns out here, we're blind until it's too late."

"Let's hope they're as bogged down as we are," Tom "Wheels" Anderson muttered, his hands tight on the controls. The tank lurched as its treads struggled to grip the muddy terrain. "This mud's like glue."

All around them, infantry trudged through the mire, their boots sinking into the muck with every step. Some used fallen branches to steady themselves, while others cursed under their breath as they hauled equipment over the treacherous ground.

The radio crackled with Lieutenant Parker's voice. "All units, advance with caution. Watch for mines and ambushes. Infantry will lead, but tanks stay close to provide cover."

"Copy that," Jack replied, his voice steady despite the tension. He turned to Joe "Quick Hands" Martinez. "Make sure we're ready for anything. Boomers first, then switch to solid shot if we run into trouble."

"Already on it, Boss," Joe said, checking the ammo rack.

The forest seemed to close in tighter as they moved deeper. The tank groaned under the strain of the terrain, its engine laboring to push through the mud. Fallen trees blocked parts of the path, forcing Tom to maneuver carefully to avoid getting stuck.

"Feels like we're crawling through a graveyard," George said, his voice hushed.

"Shut it, Grizz," Mike snapped. "We've got enough to worry about without you jinxing us."

The column pressed on, the oppressive silence broken only by the occasional snap of a branch or the distant rumble of artillery. Then, without warning, a Sherman in the middle of the column hit a mine.

The explosion was deafening, a flash of fire and smoke tearing through the forest. The force of the blast flipped the tank onto its side, its turret ripping free and landing several feet away. The screams of the crew were brief, silenced almost immediately as flames consumed the wreckage.

"Christ!" George yelled, his hands gripping the bow gun controls. "They're laying mines out here!"

"Everyone hold position!" Jack barked into the radio, his heart pounding. "Wheels, stop the tank!"

Tom slammed the controls, bringing the Iron Wolf to a halt. The forest fell silent again, save for the crackling of the burning Sherman and the distant cries of the infantry scrambling to regroup.

Jack swung his periscope toward the wreckage. The tank was a charred husk, its crew trapped inside as the fire raged. He clenched his jaw, forcing himself to focus. "Deadeye, scan the path ahead. Quick Hands, stay ready with another Boomer."

"Got it, Boss," Mike said, adjusting the turret to cover the surrounding forest.

Through the smoke, Jack saw the infantry advancing cautiously, their movements slowed by fear and the treacherous terrain. A soldier with a mine detector waved his unit forward, his body tense as he probed the ground for more hidden explosives.

"Grizzly, keep that bow gun sweeping," Jack said. "Anything moves, you light it up."

"On it," George replied, his voice steady despite the tension.

The radio crackled again. "All units, proceed with extreme caution. Engineers are clearing the path, but we're sitting ducks if the Krauts hit us now. Stay alert."

Jack keyed the mic. "Iron Wolf standing by. Let us know when it's clear."

The crew waited in tense silence, the oppressive atmosphere of the forest pressing in on them. The death of the other Sherman was a harsh reminder of how quickly things could go wrong. The Green Hell lived up to its name, and the Iron Wolf had only just begun its fight to survive.

The Iron Wolf crawled forward through the dense Hurtgen Forest, its tracks grinding against mud and broken branches. The oppressive silence returned, broken only by the occasional snap of a twig or the distant rumble of artillery. The wreckage of the flipped Sherman lay behind them, a stark reminder of the dangers hidden in the Green Hell.

Jack "Boss" Harris kept his eyes trained on the periscope, scanning the dense canopy above. Something felt off. The usual chaos of battle was missing—no gunfire, no explosions, just an eerie quiet that pressed down on the crew.

"Deadeye, anything?" Jack asked.

"Nothing yet," Mike "Deadeye" Walker replied, his hands steady on the gun controls. "But this place feels like a shooting gallery."

"Yeah," George "Grizzly" Thompson muttered from the bow gun. "And we're the ducks."

Jack was about to reply when a sharp crack echoed through the forest. He flinched instinctively as a bullet ricocheted off the turret's edge, sending sparks flying. Another shot followed, then another, the distinct sound of a sniper's rifle cutting through the silence.

"Snipers!" Jack shouted, ducking back into the turret. "Button up! Everyone inside—now!"

The crew scrambled, slamming the hatches shut as more bullets pinged off the Iron Wolf's armor. Through his periscope, Jack scanned the treetops, looking for the telltale flash of a rifle scope.

"Deadeye, get ready with a Boomer," Jack ordered. "Grizzly, keep that bow gun sweeping. If they're moving, I want them gone."

"Boomer loaded!" Joe "Quick Hands" Martinez called, his hands steady as he prepared another round.

"I see one!" Mike shouted. "Up in that tree, two o'clock! Firing!"

The Sherman's 75mm cannon roared, the high-explosive round streaking toward the suspected sniper position. The shell struck the upper branches of the tree, detonating in a deafening explosion. Wood splintered and bark flew in all directions, but the real carnage was evident in the sniper's perch. Gore and blood sprayed out, painting the surrounding foliage in a macabre tableau. What was left of the sniper's body tumbled from the branches, landing in a crumpled heap at the base of the tree.

"Got him," Mike said coldly, already scanning for another target.

"Another one! Left flank!" Jack shouted, spotting movement through the periscope.

Mike adjusted the turret, lining up the shot as another sniper fired, the round smacking into the tank's hull. The Iron Wolf's cannon fired again, the shell obliterating the tree where the sniper had taken cover. The explosion sent the man flying, his shattered body landing limp among the underbrush.

"They're picking us off one by one," George said, his voice tense as he swung the bow gun in an arc. "How many of these bastards are out there?"

"Enough to keep us pinned," Jack replied. "Deadeye, keep firing. Quick Hands, load up another Boomer. Grizzly, stay alert for movement."

The radio crackled to life with frantic reports from the other tanks in the column. "Snipers everywhere! They're targeting the commanders—stay buttoned up!"

Jack keyed the mic. "This is Iron Wolf. We're engaging. Keep your tanks tight and keep your gunners scanning. They can't hit what they can't see."

Another shot rang out, striking the Sherman behind them. The tank shuddered, but its armor held. Jack swiveled his periscope toward the source, catching a brief glimpse of a rifle barrel protruding from a camouflaged hide.

"Deadeye, three o'clock, just past that fallen log!" Jack barked.

"On it!" Mike replied, firing another high-explosive round. The shell landed squarely on the sniper's position, the explosion leaving nothing but a charred crater and fragments of wood and flesh.

The barrage of sniper fire began to slow as the Shermans systematically cleared the treetops and suspected hiding spots. The combination of bow gun fire and high-explosive rounds proved devastating, leaving the enemy no room to regroup.

"Looks like they're pulling back," Mike said, his voice steady.

"Don't count on it," Jack replied. "They've got the advantage here. Quick Hands, reload. Grizzly, keep sweeping. Deadeye, stay ready for the next shot."

The Iron Wolf pressed forward, its crew tense but focused. The Green Hell was living up to its name, and the snipers were just one of many threats lurking in the shadows.

The Iron Wolf pushed deeper into the forest, its tracks grinding through the mud and tangled roots. The wreckage of the sniper ambush lay behind them, but the oppressive atmosphere of the Hurtgen Forest remained. Every shadow, every fallen tree felt like a threat waiting to spring.

"Something's not right," Tom "Wheels" Anderson muttered, his eyes fixed on the narrow path ahead. "This place is too quiet again."

"They're out there," Jack "Boss" Harris replied from the turret, his voice low but tense. "Stay sharp. Grizzly, watch the flanks. Deadeye, be ready."

"I'm always ready," Mike "Deadeye" Walker said, his hands steady on the gun controls. "Quick Hands, what's loaded?"

"Solid shot," Joe "Quick Hands" Martinez replied. "Willie Pete on standby if we need it."

The path narrowed, forcing the column of tanks into single file. Dense trees and overgrown brush lined both sides, making it impossible to maneuver quickly. Jack's eyes scanned the terrain through his periscope, searching for anything out of place.

Then it came—the distinct crack of a Pak 40 anti-tank gun firing from the right. The shell streaked through the air, slamming into the Sherman in front of them. The tank shuddered, its armor pierced clean through. Flames erupted from the hull as the crew scrambled to escape, but the fire consumed the tank too quickly. The screams of the men inside were cut short as the ammunition cooked off, sending the turret flying in a fiery explosion.

"Pak 40, right flank!" Jack shouted. "Wheels, reverse! Get us out of its line of fire!"

Tom slammed the controls, backing the Iron Wolf into a shallow ditch. Another shell screamed past, narrowly missing the turret and slamming into a tree behind them, splintering it into jagged shards.

"Quick Hands, load Willie Pete!" Jack ordered.

Joe grabbed the white phosphorus round and loaded it into the breech. "Willie Pete loaded!" he called.

"Deadeye, smoke that gun! Blind 'em!" Jack barked.

Mike swung the turret toward the muzzle flash of the Pak 40, barely visible through the dense underbrush. He fired, the shell exploding in a burst of blinding white smoke. The phosphorus spread quickly, enveloping the enemy position in a thick, choking cloud.

"That'll keep 'em guessing," Mike said, his voice tight. "Quick Hands, reload with a Boomer!"

Joe swapped rounds with practiced speed. "Boomer loaded!"

"Wheels, hold position," Jack said. "Deadeye, aim for where that gun fired. We're taking it out."

Mike adjusted the turret, lining up the shot through the dissipating smoke. "On target… firing!"

The Sherman's cannon roared, the high-explosive round streaking toward the enemy position. The shell struck the Pak 40 directly, detonating with devastating force. The wooden frame of the gun splintered into fragments, and the crew manning it was obliterated. Limbs and torsos were torn apart, their remains scattering across the muddy ground. The blood-soaked crater where the gun had stood was all that remained.

"Target neutralized," Mike reported grimly, his voice steady despite the carnage.

Jack exhaled slowly, forcing himself to focus. "Good work. Quick Hands, reload. Grizzly, keep scanning for more threats. Wheels, stay ready to move."

The radio crackled with a report from Lieutenant Parker. "Iron Wolf, is that gun down?"

"Affirmative," Jack replied. "Pak 40 destroyed. Continuing forward."

"Good work," Parker said. "Stay alert. There could be more."

Jack turned to his crew. "We're not out of this yet. Keep your heads in the game."

The Iron Wolf pressed on, its crew tense but resolute. The ambush had been brutal, but they had survived. The Green Hell wasn't giving them an inch, and every step forward came at a cost.

The Iron Wolf crept through the dense trees of the Hurtgen Forest, its tracks grinding over roots and churned mud. The thick canopy above muffled the sounds of the distant artillery barrages, but each explosion sent vibrations through the earth, a grim reminder of the chaos surrounding them.

The radio crackled to life with an urgent message. "All units, be advised: friendly artillery is providing support. Adjust positions to avoid overlap."

Jack "Boss" Harris frowned, gripping the turret ring as he peered through his periscope. "Wheels, keep us moving, but stay sharp. Deadeye, stay ready to fire if we see anything."

"They're shooting blind out there," Mike "Deadeye" Walker muttered, his hands steady on the gun controls. "With this cover, one wrong shell could land right on us."

"Let's hope they're better at aiming than that," Tom "Wheels" Anderson said, guiding the tank carefully over a fallen log.

The forest suddenly erupted into chaos. The sharp bark of German MG42 fire came from the right, cutting down several Allied infantry in its opening burst. Soldiers scattered, diving for cover behind trees and into shell craters.

"Grizzly, bow gun! Cover the infantry!" Jack shouted.

George "Grizzly" Thompson swung the bow gun toward the muzzle flashes, opening fire. The .30 caliber sprayed the underbrush, forcing the German gunners to pull back.

"They're dug in tight!" George yelled over the din. "We're not flushing them out like this."

Jack keyed the radio. "Command, this is Iron Wolf. Requesting artillery on enemy positions, right flank!"

"Roger that, Iron Wolf. Artillery incoming. Brace for impact," came the reply.

The first shells landed moments later, sending plumes of dirt and debris into the air. The German machine-gun nest was silenced in a direct hit, but the fire didn't stop. More rounds rained down, blanketing the forest in explosions.

"Friendly fire's getting close!" Mike shouted. "They're overshooting!"

"Command, you're hitting too far back!" Jack barked into the radio. "Adjust fire before you hit our lines!"

Before a response could come, one of the artillery shells landed just ahead of the Iron Wolf. The blast threw dirt and shrapnel against the tank's hull, rattling the crew. Through his periscope, Jack saw the carnage—an Allied infantry squad caught directly in the barrage.

Men were thrown like rag dolls, their bodies shattered by the explosion. One soldier's leg was blown clean off, the jagged stump spewing blood as he writhed on the ground, screaming for a medic. Another lay motionless, his chest cavity exposed and steaming in the cold air. The survivors stumbled away, some dragging wounded comrades, their faces masks of shock and horror.

"Christ," George muttered, his hands trembling on the bow gun. "They hit our own men."

"Command, you've hit friendlies!" Jack shouted into the radio. "Cease fire immediately!"

The radio crackled back, the voice on the other end tense. "Adjusting fire. Stand by."

The artillery barrage stopped, but the damage was done. The forest was eerily quiet again, save for the cries of the wounded. Medics rushed forward, their faces pale as they worked frantically to stabilize the injured.

"Deadeye, keep scanning for threats," Jack ordered, forcing himself to stay focused. "Wheels, hold position until we're clear to move."

Inside the tank, the crew sat in tense silence, the weight of what they'd witnessed pressing down on them. Joe "Quick Hands" Martinez broke the silence, his voice barely above a whisper. "Those guys… they didn't even see it coming."

"War doesn't care," Mike replied grimly. "Wrong place, wrong time. That's all it takes."

Jack clenched his fists, his jaw tight as he tried to push the images from his mind. "We focus on the mission," he said, his voice hard. "If we don't, more of us die. That's the reality."

The Iron Wolf stayed put until the medics cleared the area, then pressed forward. The crew carried the weight of the moment with them, their resolve hardened but their spirits heavier than ever. The Green Hell of the Hurtgen Forest had claimed more lives, and the scars it left behind were more than just physical.

The Iron Wolf sat motionless in a shallow depression, its engine turned off to avoid detection. The darkness of the Hurtgen Forest was absolute, broken only by the faint glow of distant fires and the occasional flash of artillery on the horizon. The crew hunkered down inside, their breaths visible in the cold, damp air.

"Can't see a damn thing out there," George "Grizzly" Thompson muttered, his voice low as he peered out through the bow gun sight. "It's like the forest swallows the light."

"That's not the worst of it," Joe "Quick Hands" Martinez replied, leaning back against the ammo rack. "It's the sounds. You hear that? Movements, whispers. They're out there."

"Keep it together," Jack "Boss" Harris said from the turret, his voice calm but firm. "They want us to panic. That's when they get us."

The forest was alive with faint noises—the rustling of leaves, the snap of a twig, the distant murmur of voices. The enemy was close, their presence more felt than seen. The tension in the tank was suffocating, every creak of the hull amplified in the stillness.

Suddenly, a voice called out from the darkness, clear and deliberate: "Help! Please, we're American! Don't shoot!"

The words hung in the air, unnatural in their delivery. The tone was off—too rehearsed, too calculated. Jack's stomach tightened.

"Don't fall for it," he said quickly. "It's a trap."

Another voice followed, this one closer. "We're wounded! Please, we need help!"

"They're trying to bait us," Mike "Deadeye" Walker muttered, gripping the gun controls. "It's smart. They know we'll hesitate."

"Grizzly, keep that bow gun on the perimeter," Jack ordered. "Quick Hands, be ready to load at a moment's notice. Deadeye, scan for muzzle flashes or movement."

"Got it," George said, his finger resting on the trigger.

The voices continued, growing more frantic, more desperate. "Medic! We need a medic!" The cries seemed to come from all directions, bouncing off the trees and disorienting the crew.

"Smart bastards," Tom "Wheels" Anderson muttered from the driver's seat. "They know the dark works for them."

Jack nodded grimly, his eyes fixed on the periscope. "Stay quiet. If they think we're biting, they'll get sloppy."

For a long moment, the forest fell silent again. Then, a sudden burst of rifle fire broke the tension, the sharp cracks cutting through the air. The shots were close—too close.

"They're testing us," Jack said. "Deadeye, keep that gun ready."

Another voice called out, louder now. "Advance! We're falling back!" The accent was unmistakably German, but the English was clear enough to make the ruse convincing.

"I see movement," Mike said, his voice tight. "Left side, near that fallen tree. Looks like they're trying to flank us."

"Don't fire unless you're sure," Jack replied. "They might be trying to draw us out."

The minutes dragged on, the tension mounting with every sound. A branch snapped to their right, and George swung the bow gun toward the noise. He didn't fire, but his breathing was heavy.

Finally, the faint glow of a lantern appeared in the distance, bobbing through the trees. It was accompanied by more voices, the cadence of the words distinctly German despite their attempts at English.

"They're getting bolder," Joe whispered. "Boss, what do we do?"

Jack considered their options. Firing could give away their position, but doing nothing left them vulnerable. He made his decision.

"Deadeye, fire a Willie Pete round at that lantern," Jack ordered. "Blind them and force them back."

"Willie Pete loaded," Joe said, his hands moving quickly.

"On target," Mike confirmed. "Firing!"

The Sherman's cannon roared, the white phosphorus shell streaking through the trees. It detonated near the lantern, the explosion bathing the forest in blinding light and thick, choking smoke. Shouts of alarm followed, the enemy scattering as their trap unraveled.

"Nice shot," Jack said, his voice steady. "Grizzly, keep that bow gun sweeping. Wheels, be ready to move if we have to."

The forest fell quiet again, the enemy retreating into the shadows. The cries for help ceased, replaced by the distant sounds of hurried movement.

Inside the Iron Wolf, the crew sat in tense silence, their breaths shallow. The night was far from over, and the enemy was still out there, watching, waiting.

"Desperation's setting in," Jack said finally. "They're getting reckless. That makes them more dangerous. Stay sharp."

The crew nodded, their resolve hardened. The Iron Wolf was surrounded, but it was still standing, its crew ready for whatever came next in the unrelenting darkness of the Hurtgen Forest.

Chapter 7: Ambushes and Attrition

The Hurtgen Forest felt like it was closing in around the platoon as the Iron Wolf crept forward, its engine rumbling softly in the claustrophobic stillness. Jack "Boss" Harris kept his eyes locked on the periscope, scanning the dense undergrowth and narrow paths ahead. The platoon had been moving cautiously for hours, but every instinct told him they were walking into another trap.

"Feels too quiet," George "Grizzly" Thompson muttered from the bow gun. "Every time it's this quiet, something bad happens."

"You're not wrong," Mike "Deadeye" Walker replied, his hands tense on the gun controls. "They're out there. Just waiting for us to get close."

"Stay ready," Jack said, his voice low but firm. "Quick Hands, what's loaded?"

"Boomer," Joe "Quick Hands" Martinez replied. "We're ready to clear out whatever they're hiding in."

The platoon moved forward, the tanks spaced out to avoid being caught in a single concentrated strike. Infantry followed close behind, their rifles raised as they scanned the trees. The tension was palpable, every snap of a twig or rustle of leaves making hearts race.

Suddenly, the forest erupted with gunfire. A German MG42 opened up from a concealed position, its high-pitched chatter cutting through the air and forcing the infantry to dive for cover.

Moments later, a Panzerfaust streaked out from the tree line, narrowly missing the lead Sherman and exploding harmlessly against a rock.

"Contact! Dug-in positions ahead!" Jack shouted into the radio. "Deadeye, find that MG nest! Grizzly, lay down suppressing fire!"

George swung the bow gun toward the muzzle flashes, the .30-caliber spitting bullets into the underbrush. The MG42 kept firing, its rounds ricocheting off the Iron Wolf's hull.

"Got it!" Mike called out, locking onto the machine-gun position. "Firing!"

The Sherman's cannon roared, the high-explosive shell slamming into the nest. The explosion ripped through the position, sending sandbags, dirt, and bodies flying. The MG42 fell silent.

"Target neutralized," Mike said, already scanning for the next threat.

But the Germans weren't finished. More Panzerfausts streaked out from hidden positions, forcing the platoon to halt and return fire. Rifle shots cracked through the air, some striking dangerously close to the infantry huddled behind cover.

In the chaos, a German soldier emerged from the smoke, his hands raised in surrender. He shouted something in broken English, his voice desperate and terrified. Joe spotted him through the side hatch.

"Boss, he's surrendering!" Joe shouted.

Before Jack could respond, another burst of gunfire erupted from the trees. One of the infantrymen nearby panicked and fired at the German soldier, the rifle shot striking him in the chest. The man crumpled to the ground, blood pooling around him as his outstretched hand fell limp.

Joe froze, his eyes wide as he stared at the scene. "No… no, he was giving up…"

"Stay focused!" Jack snapped, his voice cutting through the shock. "We don't have time to lose it now!"

"But—" Joe started, his voice trembling.

"Quick Hands, reload!" Jack barked. "We're still in the middle of this fight!"

Joe forced himself to move, his hands shaking as he grabbed another shell and loaded it into the breech. "Boomer loaded," he said, his voice hollow.

"Deadeye, take out that Panzerfaust team!" Jack ordered.

Mike fired again, the shell detonating near a cluster of trees. The explosion sent shrapnel flying, silencing the anti-tank threat. The remaining Germans began to retreat, their positions overrun by the relentless assault.

"All units, move up and secure the area," came the voice of Lieutenant Parker over the radio. "Good work. Keep pressing forward."

Jack exhaled, the tension in his shoulders easing slightly. He turned to Joe, his tone softer now. "Quick Hands, you okay?"

Joe didn't look up. "He was surrendering," he said quietly. "He didn't even have a weapon."

"Things happen fast out here," Jack said, his voice measured. "You can't second-guess every decision. It'll get you killed."

Joe nodded numbly, but the horror of the moment lingered in his expression. The Iron Wolf pressed forward, its crew hardened by the reality of war but carrying the weight of another scar. The Hurtgen Forest continued to live up to its name, consuming everything in its path—men, machines, and their humanity alike.

The Iron Wolf rumbled to a stop on the edge of a clearing, its crew scanning the dense underbrush ahead. German bunkers were entrenched into the hillside, their positions reinforced with layers of sandbags, logs, and steel plates. The complex was a fortress, bristling with machine guns and riflemen. Allied infantry huddled behind whatever cover they could find, preparing for an assault they knew would be costly.

Jack "Boss" Harris keyed the radio. "Command, this is Iron Wolf. We're at the edge of the objective. Infantry needs support to break through. Requesting orders."

The reply came quickly. "Iron Wolf, advance with caution. Use high explosives to suppress enemy positions. Infantry will move up under your cover."

"Understood," Jack said, switching to the intercom. "Deadeye, Boomers first. Grizzly, keep that bow gun hot. Quick Hands, stay ready with a reload. Wheels, advance slow—give the infantry time to keep up."

"On it, Boss," Tom "Wheels" Anderson replied, guiding the Sherman forward.

The tank rolled into the clearing, its turret already swiveling to target the nearest bunker. The machine-gun fire started immediately, bullets pinging off the Sherman's armor. Allied infantry ducked and scrambled, using the Iron Wolf as a moving shield.

"Deadeye, hit that bunker!" Jack ordered.

Mike "Deadeye" Walker fired, the 75mm high-explosive shell slamming into the fortified position. The explosion sent sandbags and dirt flying, silencing the machine gun within.

"Boomer reloaded!" Joe "Quick Hands" Martinez called out, slamming another round into the breech.

"Deadeye, keep hitting those bunkers," Jack said. "Grizzly, watch the trenches. They'll try to flank us."

As the Iron Wolf advanced, German infantry poured out of the trenches, firing rifles and Panzerfausts at the tank and the Allied soldiers behind it. One anti-tank rocket struck a nearby Sherman, the explosion rocking the tank but failing to penetrate its armor.

"They're in the trenches!" George "Grizzly" Thompson shouted, his bow gun blazing as he cut down advancing Germans. "They're everywhere!"

Jack scanned the battlefield through his periscope. A large group of German soldiers was gathering in a trench just ahead, preparing to launch a counterattack. "Deadeye, load a shotgun round! Quick Hands, make it fast!"

Joe grabbed the canister round—a shell designed to turn the tank's cannon into a giant shotgun—and slid it into the breech. "Shotgun loaded!"

"Deadeye, trench at one o'clock. Light it up!" Jack commanded.

Mike adjusted the turret, lining up the shot. "Firing!"

The 75mm cannon roared, firing the canister round directly into the trench. Hundreds of steel balls sprayed out, ripping through the packed ranks of German soldiers. The devastation was immediate and absolute. Blood splattered the trench walls, and bodies were torn apart by the hail of projectiles. Arms, legs, and unrecognizable fragments of flesh littered the ground, the once-organized position now a scene of utter carnage.

"Trench cleared," Mike said coldly, his voice devoid of emotion.

"Good shot," Jack replied, his tone steady. "Reload and keep scanning."

The remaining German defenders began to falter, their positions overwhelmed by the combined firepower of the tanks and advancing infantry. Some tried to retreat, only to be cut down by Allied rifle fire. Others held their ground, firing desperately as the Shermans rolled closer.

"All units, push forward and secure the objective!" Lieutenant Parker's voice came over the radio.

Jack keyed the mic. "Iron Wolf, advancing."

The tank pressed on, its cannon roaring as it cleared the remaining bunkers. The infantry surged behind it, sweeping through the trenches and finishing off the last of the resistance.

By the time the fighting stopped, the clearing was a charnel house. Smoke hung heavy in the air, and the ground was soaked with blood. The Iron Wolf sat in the middle of the devastation, its steel hull scarred but unbroken.

Inside the tank, the crew sat in tense silence, the weight of what they'd done sinking in.

"Shotgun rounds don't leave much behind, do they?" Joe said quietly, his voice shaking slightly.

"No," Jack replied, his voice grim. "But they save lives—ours and theirs."

The crew nodded, their resolve hardened by the battle. The bunkers were theirs, but the cost was written in the blood and fragments left behind. The Iron Wolf had done its job, but the war in the Hurtgen Forest was far from over.

The Iron Wolf rolled to a halt at the edge of a clearing, its engine idling softly as Jack "Boss" Harris scanned the battlefield through his periscope. Smoke from the destroyed German bunkers still lingered in the air, mixing with the acrid smell of burning wood and diesel fuel. The infantry was pressing forward cautiously, checking for any hidden threats.

"All units, hold position," Lieutenant Parker's voice crackled over the radio. "Infantry is sweeping the area for any remaining resistance."

Jack acknowledged the order, his gaze shifting to the Shermans spread out behind them. The tanks were maintaining a staggered formation, their guns trained on the treeline. The tension was thick—every man in the column knew the Germans weren't finished yet.

Then it happened.

From the shadows of the forest, a German soldier stepped forward, his Panzerfaust already aimed. He fired before anyone could react, the rocket streaking toward the nearest Sherman in the column. The projectile struck the tank's rear engine compartment with devastating precision.

The explosion was deafening. The Sherman's hull shuddered as flames erupted from its engine, quickly spreading to the ammunition stored inside. Jack watched in horror as the crew scrambled to escape, their frantic movements visible through the narrow hatches.

"Get out of there!" George "Grizzly" Thompson shouted, his voice hoarse.

The burning tank became an inferno, the fire consuming the oxygen inside. One crewman managed to climb halfway out of the commander's hatch before the tank's ammunition detonated. The blast sent the turret flying into the air, a fireball erupting from the hull. The force of the explosion threw the crewman clear, his lifeless body tumbling across the ground.

Shrapnel from the explosion tore through the nearby area, embedding itself in the trees and ground. Jack winced as a large piece of twisted metal landed just a few feet from the Iron Wolf. Through his periscope, he could see the devastation—the remains of the Sherman's crew scattered across the clearing, their bodies torn apart by the blast.

"Christ," Mike "Deadeye" Walker muttered, his voice tight with shock. "They didn't stand a chance."

"We need to move!" Jack barked, snapping himself out of the moment. "Wheels, back us up! Deadeye, find that shooter! Grizzly, cover the infantry!"

Tom "Wheels" Anderson slammed the controls, reversing the Iron Wolf into a more defensible position. Mike swung the turret toward the treeline, searching for the Panzerfaust team. The bow gun roared to life as George laid down suppressing fire, keeping the advancing infantry safe.

"I see him!" Mike shouted. "Two o'clock, near that broken tree!"

"Quick Hands, load a Boomer!" Jack ordered.

"Boomer loaded!" Joe "Quick Hands" Martinez replied, his hands moving quickly despite the tension.

"Take him out, Deadeye!" Jack commanded.

Mike fired, the high-explosive round streaking toward the target. The shell detonated near the Panzerfaust team, the blast reducing them to a cloud of smoke, debris, and broken bodies. The immediate threat was neutralized, but the burning Sherman remained a haunting sight.

The crew of the Iron Wolf sat in stunned silence for a moment, the gravity of what they had just witnessed sinking in. The destroyed Sherman was now little more than a smoldering husk, its twisted metal frame a testament to the brutal efficiency of the German weapon.

"They were just kids," Joe said softly, his voice barely audible. "They didn't even get a chance to fight back."

Jack took a deep breath, forcing himself to stay focused. "It could've been us," he said. "It almost was. That's why we stay sharp. That's why we keep moving."

The crew nodded, their resolve hardening. The Iron Wolf pressed forward, leaving the burning tank behind as a grim reminder of the stakes they faced. In the Hurtgen Forest, survival was never guaranteed.

The Iron Wolf ground forward, its engine groaning as it climbed over thick roots and churned mud. The Hurtgen Forest's terrain was relentless, each yard gained a battle against nature itself. Visibility was limited by the dense canopy above and the smoke still hanging in the air from the earlier bombardment.

Jack "Boss" Harris kept his eyes trained on the periscope, scanning the narrow path ahead. The Germans had proven their determination time and again, and he knew they wouldn't let up now. "Grizzly, keep watching for movement. Deadeye, you're on overwatch. Wheels, ease us forward—slow and steady."

"Got it, Boss," Tom "Wheels" Anderson replied, his hands steady on the controls.

"Path looks worse than a cow trail," George "Grizzly" Thompson muttered from the bow gun. "Might as well have painted a big bullseye on us."

"Then make sure no one gets close," Jack shot back. "And watch for anything that looks out of place. Mines, tripwires—if it doesn't belong, call it out."

The crew was tense but focused. Small-arms fire crackled sporadically from the treeline, bullets pinging harmlessly off the Sherman's thick armor. Allied infantry huddled behind the tank, using it as mobile cover as they advanced cautiously.

"Boss, we've got movement on the left!" George called out, swiveling the bow gun toward a cluster of trees.

"Hold fire," Jack ordered, peering through the periscope. The shadows played tricks on his eyes, but there—just barely visible—was a German soldier darting between the trees, his rifle raised.

"Deadeye, hit that treeline!" Jack barked.

Mike "Deadeye" Walker fired, the 75mm cannon roaring as the high-explosive round slammed into the trees. The blast shredded branches and sent dirt flying, silencing the enemy fire from that direction.

"Nice shot," Jack said. "Grizzly, keep scanning."

The tank lurched as it moved over uneven ground. Tom slowed, his hands tightening on the controls. "Boss, we've got some nasty terrain up ahead. Looks like a minefield—nothing marked, but I don't like the look of it."

"Grizzly, what do you see?" Jack asked.

George leaned forward, his sharp eyes studying the path. The ground ahead was littered with debris—fallen branches, jagged rocks, and patches of disturbed soil. "It's a damn mine maze," he muttered. "Those bastards knew we'd come this way."

"Deadeye, hold fire. Wheels, back us up a bit," Jack ordered. "Grizzly, guide us through. If you see anything suspicious, call it out."

George nodded, taking a deep breath. "Alright. Wheels, give me a slow crawl. Let's hope I'm as lucky as I am handsome."

The Iron Wolf crept forward, each movement deliberate and cautious. George kept his eyes fixed on the ground, his hands steady on the bow gun controls. He called out directions with precision, steering the Sherman away from any patches of disturbed soil or exposed metal that could indicate a mine.

"Left a bit, Wheels. Easy now. Good. Okay, straighten out," George said, his voice calm despite the tension.

The tank jolted as one of its tracks rolled over a hidden branch, snapping it with a loud crack. The crew froze, every muscle tense as they waited for the sound of an explosion. Nothing came.

"False alarm," George said, exhaling sharply. "Keep going, Wheels."

The small-arms fire continued sporadically, but the Iron Wolf pressed on, its hull impervious to the scattered rifle shots. Behind the tank, infantry followed in a tight formation, their boots squelching in the mud.

"Almost through," George said, his eyes scanning the final stretch of the treacherous path. "Another fifty yards, and we're clear."

As the tank moved past the last patch of disturbed soil, a sudden burst of machine-gun fire erupted from the treeline ahead. The infantry scattered, diving for cover as bullets ricocheted off the Sherman's armor.

"Contact! Front!" Jack shouted. "Grizzly, suppress that fire! Deadeye, target the nest!"

George opened up with the bow gun, his rounds spraying the treeline and forcing the German gunners to keep their heads down. Mike swung the turret, lining up a shot.

"Boomer loaded!" Joe "Quick Hands" Martinez called.

Mike fired, the high-explosive shell slamming into the machine-gun position. The explosion silenced the fire, leaving only smoke and the distant echoes of battle.

"Clear," Mike said, his voice steady.

"Good work," Jack replied. "Grizzly, nice navigation. Wheels, take us to the next rally point."

"Glad we're out of that mess," Tom muttered as he guided the Sherman onto firmer ground.

The Iron Wolf rolled forward, leaving the minefield and ambush behind. The crew remained vigilant, knowing the fight was far from over. In the Hurtgen Forest, every inch gained came at a cost, and the Iron Wolf was determined to keep moving, no matter the odds.

The Iron Wolf sat motionless in a shallow hollow, its engine off to conserve fuel. The Hurtgen Forest wrapped around it like a suffocating blanket, the towering trees casting long shadows that merged into the pitch-black night. Smoke from the day's battles still hung heavy in the air, mingling with the acrid stench of burned metal, oil, and blood.

Inside the Sherman, the crew huddled in silence, their exhaustion palpable. Jack "Boss" Harris sat in the turret, his eyes scanning the darkness through the periscope. Every snap of a branch or rustle of leaves outside set his nerves on edge.

"Quiet," George "Grizzly" Thompson muttered from the bow gun, his voice barely above a whisper. "Too damn quiet. I'd almost rather hear gunfire."

"No, you wouldn't," Mike "Deadeye" Walker replied from his seat at the gun controls, his tone flat. "We've had enough of that for one day."

Tom "Wheels" Anderson leaned back in his seat, his arms crossed tightly over his chest. "We're out of rations, Boss," he said quietly. "Haven't eaten since yesterday morning."

Jack nodded grimly. "I know. We'll scavenge when we can, but for now, we sit tight. Movement at night is asking for a Panzerfaust to the face."

Joe "Quick Hands" Martinez shifted uncomfortably, his stomach growling audibly. "Feels like we've been running on fumes for days," he said. "No food, barely any sleep. How the hell are we supposed to keep going?"

Jack sighed, his voice low but steady. "We keep going because we have to. There's no other option."

Outside, the distant rumble of artillery echoed through the forest, a low, ominous sound that seemed to vibrate through the earth. The crew sat in silence, listening to the endless barrage, each man lost in his own thoughts.

"This place…" George said after a long pause. "It's like it's alive. Like it wants to kill us."

"It's not the forest," Mike replied. "It's the bastards hiding in it. They know every inch of this place, and they're not giving it up without a fight."

"Doesn't feel like a fight," Joe said softly. "Feels like we're just surviving. Barely."

Jack glanced at his crew, their faces lit only by the faint glow of a small flashlight George had propped up near the ammo rack. They were worn down, their uniforms caked with mud and blood, their eyes hollow with fatigue.

"We'll get through this," Jack said, his voice firm despite the doubt gnawing at him. "We've made it this far, haven't we?"

"Yeah," Tom muttered. "But how much farther can we go? How many more Shermans do we lose before it's us burning out there?"

The words hung heavy in the air, a truth none of them wanted to confront. The Iron Wolf had survived countless engagements, but every battle took its toll, and the Hurtgen Forest seemed determined to grind them down to nothing.

Outside, the artillery grew louder, the distant booms punctuated by the occasional sharp crack of small-arms fire. Jack gripped the turret ring tightly, his knuckles white. He couldn't let his crew see his fear, couldn't let them know he shared their doubts.

"Get some rest," he said finally. "We've got a long day ahead of us."

"Rest," George scoffed. "In this place? With those Krauts creeping around out there?"

"Just try," Jack said. "We'll take shifts. Deadeye, you're up first. Keep an eye on the perimeter."

Mike nodded, adjusting his seat to face the turret controls. "Got it, Boss."

One by one, the crew settled into uneasy positions, their bodies too tired to care about comfort. The Sherman's steel walls offered little warmth, and the cold night air seeped in, making their breaths visible in the dim light.

As the others drifted into fitful sleep, Jack remained awake, his eyes scanning the treeline through the periscope. The artillery fire continued in the distance, a grim reminder that the war was far from over. For now, the Iron Wolf was safe, but the forest had already claimed so much, and Jack knew it wouldn't stop until it had taken everything.

"We'll make it," he whispered to himself, though the words felt hollow. "We have to."

The night stretched on, long and unforgiving, as the crew of the Iron Wolf braced themselves for whatever horrors the next day would bring.

Chapter 8: Surviving the Hurtgen Forest

The Iron Wolf idled at the edge of the treeline, its engine rumbling softly as the tank company prepared for a desperate push to break through the German defenses. The morning light struggled to pierce the thick canopy of the Hurtgen Forest, casting everything in a pale, gray gloom. Allied infantry huddled behind trees and rocks, their faces drawn and pale, their eyes fixed on the enemy positions ahead.

Jack "Boss" Harris surveyed the battlefield through his periscope. The Germans had fortified the ridge ahead with machine-gun nests, trenches, and barbed wire. It was a killing field, and every man on the Allied side knew it. But breaking through this line was their only chance to escape the forest's relentless grip.

"Listen up," Jack said, his voice steady as he addressed the crew. "This is it. We're the spearhead, which means we go in first and hit them hard. Deadeye, Boomers to start. Quick Hands, keep us stocked. Grizzly, cover the infantry. Wheels, keep us moving no matter what."

"You got it, Boss," Tom "Wheels" Anderson replied, gripping the controls tightly.

"Hope you're ready to get dirty," George "Grizzly" Thompson muttered, his hands already on the bow gun. "This is gonna be ugly."

The radio crackled with Lieutenant Parker's voice. "All units, this is it. Advance on my command. Tanks lead the way. Infantry, follow closely and stick to cover. Godspeed."

Jack keyed the mic. "Iron Wolf, ready to move."

A tense silence hung over the forest, broken only by the distant rumble of artillery. Then, Parker's voice came through: "Go!"

The Iron Wolf surged forward, its tracks tearing through the mud as the tank company advanced in a loose formation. Allied infantry followed closely, their boots splashing through puddles and slick mud as they moved toward the enemy lines.

The Germans responded immediately. MG42 machine guns opened up from the ridge, their high-pitched chatter cutting through the air like a buzz saw. Bullets ripped into the advancing infantry, mowing down entire squads in seconds. Men fell screaming, their bodies riddled with rounds, their blood soaking into the forest floor.

"Grizzly, suppress those machine guns!" Jack shouted.

George opened fire with the bow gun, spraying the ridge with .30-caliber rounds. The Iron Wolf's cannon roared as Mike "Deadeye" Walker fired a high-explosive shell at one of the nests. The blast tore through the sandbags and sent the German gunners flying, their bodies broken and lifeless.

"Boomer reloaded!" Joe "Quick Hands" Martinez called out.

"Deadeye, hit the next one!" Jack ordered.

Mike fired again, the shell obliterating another machine-gun position. But the Germans weren't giving up. More fire erupted from the trenches, cutting down the infantry as they struggled to advance.

"Boss, they're tearing us apart!" George yelled, his voice tight with anger. "The ground's covered in bodies."

Jack's jaw tightened as he saw what George meant. The path ahead was littered with the dead and dying, Allied soldiers who hadn't made it past the initial line of fire. But there was no stopping now.

"Wheels, keep us moving," Jack said, his voice hard. "We've got to break through."

Tom hesitated for a moment, then pushed the tank forward. The Iron Wolf lurched as its tracks rolled over the bodies in its path, the weight of the Sherman crushing them into the mud. The sound was sickening—a mix of crunching bones and squelching flesh—but there was no other way.

"Jesus," Joe muttered, his face pale as he avoided looking at the periscope. "We're rolling over our own guys…"

"It's them or us," Jack said, forcing the words out. "We've got to get through."

The Iron Wolf pressed on, its cannon firing relentlessly as it cleared the way for the remaining infantry. One by one, the German machine-gun nests fell silent, their crews either killed or forced to retreat. The barbed wire was flattened under the tank's weight, creating a path for the soldiers behind them.

"All units, keep pushing!" Parker's voice came over the radio, filled with urgency. "The line is breaking!"

The Iron Wolf crested the ridge, its crew battered but determined. The Germans were pulling back, their defenses crumbling under the relentless assault. For the first time in days, the crew felt a glimmer of hope.

"Deadeye, keep firing. Grizzly, watch for stragglers. Wheels, don't stop until we're clear," Jack said, his voice steady.

The tank pressed forward, its tracks leaving a trail of mud, blood, and broken bodies. The Hurtgen Forest had exacted a heavy toll, but the Iron Wolf was still standing, still fighting. And for now, that was enough.

The Iron Wolf crested the ridge, its engine roaring as the crew pushed forward. Ahead, the final line of German defenses came into view—a mix of trenches, fortified bunkers, and a deadly threat sitting in the center of it all: a Panther tank.

Jack "Boss" Harris spotted the Panther through his periscope. The sleek, angular hull and long 75mm gun made it a formidable opponent, more than capable of knocking out a Sherman at range. It was parked behind a sandbagged position, its turret swiveling slowly to track the advancing Allied tanks.

"Panther tank, dead ahead!" Jack barked into the intercom. "Deadeye, it's out of our league at this range. We need to flank it."

"Damn," Mike "Deadeye" Walker muttered. "One good shot from that thing, and we're toast."

"Wheels, take us left," Jack ordered. "We'll use the trees for cover. Quick Hands, load a Super round. We're going to need it."

Joe "Quick Hands" Martinez nodded, his hands moving swiftly to retrieve the HVAP (High-Velocity Armor-Piercing) round. The tungsten-cored shell was their best chance against the Panther's thick armor. "Super loaded!" he called.

The Iron Wolf veered left, moving into the treeline to avoid the Panther's direct line of fire. The radio crackled with frantic reports from other Shermans in the platoon.

"This is Hammer Three! Panther hit us! We're bailing out!"
"Hammer Two, hold position! We're taking fire from infantry on the right!"

Jack ignored the chatter, his focus on maneuvering his tank into a position to strike. "Grizzly, keep that bow gun ready. If they've got infantry covering it, I don't want them sneaking up on us."

"Got it," George "Grizzly" Thompson replied, his eyes scanning the dense underbrush.

The Panther fired, its cannon roaring as it sent a shell streaking across the battlefield. Jack watched in horror as the round struck a Sherman to their right. The tank exploded, its turret flying off in a fiery arc. Smoke and flames poured from the wreckage, and Jack could see the silhouettes of the crew trying to escape the inferno.

"Move, Wheels! Get us into position before it turns on us!" Jack shouted.

Tom "Wheels" Anderson pushed the Sherman forward, weaving through the trees as the Iron Wolf closed the distance. The Panther's turret began to swivel in their direction, its gun glinting in the pale light.

"Deadeye, be ready!" Jack called out. "Quick Hands, make sure that Super's ready to go."

"It's locked and loaded," Joe said, his voice steady despite the tension.

The Iron Wolf broke from the treeline, emerging on the Panther's exposed flank. The German crew hadn't expected the maneuver, and the turret struggled to rotate fast enough to track them.

"Deadeye, now!" Jack ordered.

Mike aimed carefully, lining up the shot at the Panther's side armor. "Firing!" he shouted.

The HVAP round blasted from the Iron Wolf's cannon, the tungsten-core projectile striking the Panther's hull with incredible force. The shell penetrated the armor with a sharp crack, reaching the tank's ammunition stores.

The Panther exploded in a massive fireball, the turret ripping free from the hull and flying several feet into the air before crashing back down. Shards of metal and body parts rained across the battlefield, the remains of the German crew obliterated in the blast. The air filled with the acrid smell of burning fuel and charred flesh.

"Target destroyed!" Mike called out, his voice filled with a mix of relief and adrenaline.

"Good shot!" Jack said, his tone sharp. "Grizzly, watch for any infantry trying to regroup. Wheels, move us into cover before someone else targets us."

As the Iron Wolf backed into the treeline, the remaining German defenders began to retreat, their morale shattered by the loss of their Panther. Allied infantry surged forward, clearing the trenches and capturing stragglers.

Inside the tank, the crew allowed themselves a moment to breathe. The destruction they had wrought was horrific, but it had saved countless lives.

"Super round lived up to its name," Joe said, his voice shaky but relieved.

"Damn right it did," Mike replied, a rare grin crossing his face. "One less Panther to worry about."

Jack nodded, his expression grim. "We're not out of this yet. Reload and get ready. The Germans aren't done, and neither are we."

The Iron Wolf moved forward again, leaving the smoking wreckage of the Panther behind. The forest was still alive with the sounds of battle, but the crew knew they had struck a decisive blow. In the Hurtgen Forest, every victory was hard-won, and the cost was always high.

The Iron Wolf rumbled forward, its tracks grinding over the churned-up earth as the Hurtgen Forest began to thin out. The dense canopy that had suffocated them for weeks gave way to patches of open sky, the pale light of the overcast day breaking through the branches. Smoke from burning trees and vehicles still lingered, a grim reminder of the cost of their advance.

"All units, this is Command," the radio crackled. "The German line is broken. Push forward and regroup in the open field past the ridge. Good work."

Jack "Boss" Harris slumped slightly against the turret ring, his grip on the periscope loosening for the first time in hours. "You heard him, Wheels. Take us forward. Let's see some daylight."

Tom "Wheels" Anderson nodded, his hands steady on the controls despite the fatigue etched into his face. "About damn time. I was starting to think we'd never get out of this place."

As the Iron Wolf moved, the forest thinned further, the dense treeline giving way to open terrain. The air felt different—less oppressive—but the relief was tempered by the scenes of devastation they left behind. Wrecked tanks, abandoned artillery, and countless bodies littered the battlefield. The ground was scarred by craters and stained with blood, a grim testament to the battle they had fought.

"Grizzly, what's the rear look like?" Jack asked.

George "Grizzly" Thompson scanned the path behind them through the bow gun sight. "Looks clear, Boss. What's left of the Krauts are running for it."

"Let them go," Jack said. "They've had enough, and so have we."

The radio crackled with scattered chatter from other tank crews and infantry. Reports of losses, requests for medics, and muted cheers at finally breaking free of the forest filled the airwaves. The Hurtgen had been a nightmare, and though they had survived, it was clear many hadn't.

"Deadeye, any movement ahead?" Jack asked.

Mike "Deadeye" Walker adjusted the turret slightly, scanning the horizon through the gun sight. "Nothing hostile. Just open ground and a few scattered trees. Feels weird not having someone shooting at us."

Joe "Quick Hands" Martinez leaned back against the ammo rack, his helmet tipped forward over his face. "I don't care what's out there. As long as it's not this damn forest, I'm good."

The Iron Wolf crested the ridge, and for the first time in days, the crew had an unobstructed view of the terrain ahead. A wide, open field stretched out before them, dotted with patches of grass and the occasional farmstead. Allied troops and vehicles were already regrouping, their shapes small and distant against the expanse.

"Boss, you seeing this?" Tom said, his voice tinged with disbelief. "We're out. We made it."

Jack exhaled slowly, his eyes scanning the scene. "Yeah. We made it."

But the relief was short-lived. The radio came alive with reports of casualties and losses. Entire platoons had been wiped out in the push, and the survivors were battered and broken. The Hurtgen had taken its toll, and the cost of their victory weighed heavily on everyone who had made it out.

"Think it was worth it?" Joe asked quietly, his voice barely audible.

Jack didn't answer immediately. He glanced at his crew—tired, filthy, and hollow-eyed. "I don't know," he said finally. "But we're still here. That has to mean something."

The Iron Wolf rolled into the clearing where the other tanks and infantry had gathered. Medics moved between the wounded, their expressions grim as they worked to stabilize the worst cases. Engineers inspected damaged vehicles, their tools clanking in the heavy silence. The air was thick with exhaustion and muted grief.

George broke the silence inside the tank. "We made it through, but it feels like we left part of ourselves back there."

"Because we did," Mike said flatly. "You don't go through something like that and come out the same."

Jack nodded slowly. "Let's get some rest while we can. We've still got a war to win."

The crew didn't argue. As the Iron Wolf came to a halt, they slumped into their seats, their bodies and minds finally giving in to the fatigue. Outside, the open terrain stretched out before them, a stark contrast to the suffocating forest they had fought so hard to escape.

Relief had come at last, but it carried a heavy cost—a cost the crew of the Iron Wolf would carry with them for the rest of their lives.

The Iron Wolf sat parked on the edge of the clearing, its engine finally silent. Around it, the remnants of the platoon were regrouping. Medics worked tirelessly to treat the wounded, and supply trucks rolled in with much-needed fuel, ammunition, and rations. The smell of burning oil and the metallic tang of blood lingered in the air, but for the first time in weeks, the crew had a moment to breathe.

Jack "Boss" Harris climbed out of the turret, his boots hitting the ground with a heavy thud. He stretched his arms, feeling the ache in his shoulders and back from days spent cramped inside the Sherman. Tom "Wheels" Anderson followed, wiping the grime from his face with a rag.

"Feels weird being out in the open," Tom said, leaning against the tank. "After that forest, I almost feel exposed."

"Better exposed than trapped," Jack replied, lighting a cigarette. He took a long drag, the smoke curling around his face before disappearing into the cold air. "We earned this break."

Tom nodded, his gaze drifting toward the other tanks in the clearing. Many were damaged, their armor scarred and blackened. Some had their turrets removed for repairs, while others were little more than burned-out husks.

"We lost a lot of good men back there," Tom said quietly.

Jack exhaled slowly, watching the smoke from his cigarette dissipate. "That's war," he said, his voice low. "We've been here before, remember?"

Tom glanced at Jack, a faint smile tugging at the corner of his mouth. "North Africa," he said. "El Alamein. You remember that?"

"How could I forget?" Jack replied, shaking his head. "We were green as hell, didn't know a damn thing about tank warfare. First battle, we barely made it out alive."

Tom chuckled softly, though there was little humor in it. "I remember stalling in the middle of the field, the whole column yelling at me to get moving. Thought I was done for."

"And then you got the engine running just in time," Jack said, smiling faintly. "Pulled us out of that mess like a pro. That's when I knew you'd be my driver."

Tom shrugged, his grin fading. "We thought it was bad back then. Didn't know what was waiting for us in Europe."

Jack nodded, his expression grim. "Yeah. El Alamein was brutal, but it wasn't like this. Hurtgen was… different. Felt like we were fighting the forest as much as the Krauts."

"Still are," Tom said. "Even out here, it's like the place follows you."

The two men fell silent, each lost in their own thoughts. Around them, the camp was bustling with activity. Mechanics worked on the damaged tanks, their tools clanking against the steel hulls. Soldiers huddled around fires, sharing what little food and warmth they could find.

George "Grizzly" Thompson and Mike "Deadeye" Walker sat on the side of the tank, passing a canteen of water back and forth. Joe "Quick Hands" Martinez was stretched out on the ground nearby, his helmet over his face as he tried to steal a few moments of rest.

"Grizz, you still got that lucky coin?" Mike asked, his voice light despite the exhaustion in his eyes.

George pulled a battered coin from his pocket, holding it up for Mike to see. "Always," he said. "Rubbed it before every battle, and we're still here, aren't we?"

"Barely," Joe muttered from under his helmet. "Don't think your coin's doing much for our rations."

George grinned, flipping the coin in the air. "Maybe it's saving it for the big stuff."

Jack watched them from a distance, a faint smile playing on his lips. Moments like this—quiet, shared moments of camaraderie—were rare, and he knew they wouldn't last. The worst of the war was still ahead, but for now, they had this.

"Think we'll ever stop fighting?" Tom asked, breaking the silence.

Jack didn't answer right away. He took another drag of his cigarette, letting the question linger in the cold air. "I don't know," he said finally. "But until we do, we fight to survive. That's all we can do."

Tom nodded, his eyes fixed on the horizon. "Yeah. Guess that's all we've ever done."

The two men stood in silence as the camp settled into an uneasy rhythm. The Iron Wolf, battered but still standing, loomed behind them like a silent sentinel, a reminder of the battles they'd fought and the ones still to come.

The Iron Wolf sat among the other tanks, its steel hull streaked with mud, ash, and the scars of countless battles. Around the crew, the camp bustled with controlled chaos. Medics tended to the wounded, mechanics worked tirelessly to repair the damaged vehicles, and soldiers packed up supplies in preparation for the next move. The air was heavy with exhaustion, but there was an undercurrent of determination.

Jack "Boss" Harris leaned against the side of the Sherman, his arms crossed as he watched the activity around him. The respite had been brief, but he knew it wouldn't last. The war waited for no one.

The radio crackled to life, the sharp voice of Lieutenant Parker breaking through the static. "All units, listen up. New orders just came down. We're regrouping and pushing toward Belgium. The Germans are digging in, and we need to keep the pressure on. Be ready to move at first light."

Jack straightened, his jaw tightening. He keyed the mic. "Iron Wolf copies. What's the objective?"

"Advance to the Ardennes," Parker replied. "The brass is planning something big. For now, get your crew ready and fall in with the column. Parker out."

Jack clicked off the mic and turned to his crew. "You heard him. Pack it up. We're moving out."

Tom "Wheels" Anderson groaned from where he sat on a crate, wiping oil from his hands. "Can't we catch a break? We just got out of one hellhole, and now they're sending us into another."

"War doesn't care about breaks," Jack said. "You know that."

Mike "Deadeye" Walker climbed down from the turret, rolling his shoulders. "Belgium, huh? Think we'll get a proper fight this time, or is it just more ambushes and mud?"

"Probably both," George "Grizzly" Thompson said, tossing his empty canteen aside. "At least it's not this damn forest. I've had enough trees for a lifetime."

Joe "Quick Hands" Martinez, who had been repacking the ammunition stores, looked up with a grimace. "Belgium means cold, though. Real cold. I can feel it in my bones already."

Jack smirked faintly, though there was little humor in his expression. "It's war. Cold, hot, mud, or snow—it doesn't matter. We do the job."

The crew got to work, each man falling into their routine despite the weight of fatigue pressing down on them. Tom checked the tank's tracks and engine, ensuring they were ready for another long march. Mike cleaned the gun sights, muttering under his breath about how much worse the next campaign could be. George loaded the bow gun and kept a wary eye on the perimeter, his nerves still raw from the ambushes in the forest. Joe double-checked the ammo racks, his hands steady despite the tension in his shoulders.

As they prepared, the camp began to transform. Tents were taken down, vehicles were fueled, and soldiers formed into tight, determined groups. The Allied forces were moving out, their sights set on the next objective.

"Boss," Tom called from the driver's hatch. "Tracks look good. Engine's purring like a kitten. We're ready to roll."

Jack nodded, climbing onto the turret and taking his usual spot. "Let's hope she holds. We'll need every ounce of strength she's got for what's coming."

The crew settled into their positions, the interior of the Sherman feeling both familiar and suffocating. The roar of engines filled the air as the column began to move, the tanks and trucks kicking up mud and debris as they rolled out of the clearing.

Through his periscope, Jack saw the forest shrinking behind them. It was a grim reminder of what they'd endured, but also a symbol of what they had survived. Ahead lay Belgium and another chapter of the war, filled with unknown challenges and dangers.

"Deadeye, keep an eye out," Jack said. "Grizzly, watch the flanks. Quick Hands, keep us stocked. Wheels, stay steady. This isn't over."

"It never is," George muttered, gripping the bow gun controls.

As the Iron Wolf joined the column, the crew braced themselves for the road ahead. The

Hurtgen Forest was behind them, but the war stretched endlessly before them. Belgium awaited,

and with it, a new campaign that would test their resolve once more.

Chapter 9: The Battle of the Bulge

The Iron Wolf rumbled into the frozen forests of the Ardennes, its steel hull coated in frost from the biting cold. Snow blanketed the ground, muffling the sound of the tank's tracks as it moved cautiously along the narrow, icy roads. The air was bitter, every breath visible as a pale cloud. Around the Sherman, Allied troops moved in subdued silence, their faces pale and drawn from the relentless cold.

"Feels like we've marched into a freezer," George "Grizzly" Thompson muttered from the bow gun, his gloved hands rubbing together for warmth. "How the hell are we supposed to fight in this?"

"Carefully," Jack "Boss" Harris replied from the turret, his eyes scanning the treeline through his periscope. "Keep your focus on the job. The cold's not going anywhere."

"Neither are the Krauts," Mike "Deadeye" Walker said from the gunner's seat. "This feels wrong, Boss. Too quiet."

"You're not wrong," Jack said. "Stay sharp. Quick Hands, what's loaded?"

"Boomer," Joe "Quick Hands" Martinez replied, his voice slightly muffled by the scarf wrapped around his face. "Super's ready if we need it."

The platoon advanced cautiously, the tanks spaced out to avoid presenting an easy target. Snow fell softly from the overcast sky, the peaceful scene belying the chaos about to unfold. Suddenly, the radio crackled with a frantic transmission.

"All units, be advised! Enemy forces are advancing! Artillery incoming—brace yourselves!"

Before Jack could respond, the first shells hit. The artillery barrage was deafening, a relentless series of explosions that shook the ground and tore through the frozen forest. Trees splintered and fell, their branches shattering like glass under the force of the blasts. The Iron Wolf shuddered violently as a shell exploded nearby, sending a shower of snow and dirt over the tank.

"Hold steady!" Jack shouted, gripping the turret ring tightly as the Sherman rocked under the force of the barrage. "Wheels, keep us moving! We're sitting ducks if we stop!"

"I'm trying, Boss!" Tom "Wheels" Anderson yelled, his hands fighting to keep the tank on the icy road. The tracks slipped and groaned as they clawed for traction on the frozen ground.

Another shell landed even closer, the shockwave slamming into the Iron Wolf like a sledgehammer. Inside, the crew was thrown against their seats, the interior filled with the sound of rattling steel and the acrid smell of cordite.

"Christ, they're zeroing in on us!" George yelled, his voice tight with fear and adrenaline.

"Grizzly, watch the flanks! Deadeye, be ready to fire!" Jack barked. "Quick Hands, make sure we're stocked!"

Outside, the platoon was in disarray. Infantry scrambled for cover, diving into shell craters and behind trees as the artillery rained down. A nearby Sherman took a direct hit, its hull erupting in a ball of fire. The turret blew off, landing several yards away with a sickening thud. The screams of the crew inside were drowned out by the roar of the flames.

"They're tearing us apart!" Joe shouted, his hands fumbling with the next round. "What do we do, Boss?"

"We push through!" Jack replied, his voice firm. "Deadeye, keep scanning for targets. Wheels, get us out of this kill zone!"

The Iron Wolf powered forward, its tracks grinding through the snow and debris. Shells continued to fall, some landing so close that the concussive force made the crew's ears ring. The tank lurched as a tree collapsed onto its hull, the heavy branches scraping against the steel before sliding off.

"Boss, we're almost clear of the barrage!" Tom called, his voice strained as he fought to keep the tank moving.

"Good. Once we're out, find cover and regroup," Jack ordered.

The artillery barrage began to slacken as the Iron Wolf pushed forward, finally reaching the edge of the bombardment zone. Jack scanned the area through his periscope, his heart pounding as he took in the scene. The battlefield was a hellscape of craters, shattered trees, and burning vehicles. The snow was stained red with blood, and the air was thick with smoke and the smell of death.

"Deadeye, anything?" Jack asked.

"Nothing yet," Mike replied, his voice cold. "But they're out there. I can feel it."

Jack keyed the radio. "Iron Wolf to command. We're clear of the barrage. Awaiting further orders."

The reply crackled back. "Hold position and prepare for enemy contact. They're coming."

Jack exhaled, his breath visible in the freezing air. "You heard him," he said to the crew. "Get ready. This fight's just getting started."

The Iron Wolf settled into position, its crew tense but determined. The Battle of the Bulge had begun, and the frozen forests of the Ardennes were about to become the stage for one of the most desperate battles of the war.

The Iron Wolf crept through the frozen terrain of the Ardennes, its engine groaning in the bitter cold. The subzero temperatures turned every movement into a chore, the freezing air biting through the steel hull and into the crew's bones. Frost coated the tank's exterior, and even inside, their breaths hung visibly in the air.

Jack "Boss" Harris adjusted his helmet, his gloved hands trembling slightly as he peered through the periscope. Snow crunched under the Sherman's tracks, the sound unnaturally loud in the eerie silence of the forest.

"How are we supposed to fight in this?" George "Grizzly" Thompson muttered from the bow gun. His voice was hoarse, his lips cracked from the cold. "Feels like my fingers are gonna snap off."

"Keep moving, keep warm," Jack replied. "And stop complaining. You think the Krauts are having a better time?"

"They're probably freezing too," Joe "Quick Hands" Martinez said, rubbing his hands together. "But they've had practice. We're just trying not to freeze solid out here."

"Focus," Jack snapped. "Deadeye, what do you see?"

Mike "Deadeye" Walker adjusted the gun sight, his hands steady despite the chill. "Nothing yet," he replied. "But it's too damn quiet."

The radio crackled, breaking the silence. "Iron Wolf, this is Hammer Two. We've got a Panther ahead of us, moving through the trees. Be advised, it's hunting."

Jack keyed the mic. "Copy that, Hammer Two. We'll flank it. Keep it busy."

"Wheels, take us left," Jack ordered. "Stay slow and keep us in the treeline. Grizzly, watch for infantry. Quick Hands, load solid shot. Deadeye, get ready."

Joe grabbed the armor-piercing round, his hands stiff from the cold. "Solid shot loaded," he said, slamming the breech shut.

Tom "Wheels" Anderson guided the Sherman carefully through the snow, the treads crunching over icy patches as they maneuvered toward the reported Panther's position. Every nerve in the crew was on edge, their breath shallow as they scanned the forest for movement.

"There!" Mike shouted. "Panther, dead ahead! Looks like it hasn't seen us yet."

The Panther sat partially concealed behind a fallen tree, its turret swiveling slowly as its crew searched for targets. The thick armor and angular design made it an intimidating sight, even from a distance.

"Wheels, move us closer," Jack said, his voice tight. "We need a shot at its rear."

The Iron Wolf crept forward, staying just inside the cover of the trees. The Panther remained oblivious, its attention focused on the distant Allied column.

"Grizzly, anything on the flanks?" Jack asked.

"Clear so far," George replied, his voice tense. "But they could have infantry crawling around."

Jack nodded. "Deadeye, line up the shot. Wait for my order."

Mike adjusted the gun sights, the Panther's rear armor coming into focus. The thick steel of its front and sides would be difficult to penetrate, but the rear was a known weak point. They just needed the right angle.

"On target," Mike said, his voice steady.

The Panther began to move, its engine roaring as it repositioned itself. Jack seized the moment. "Fire!"

The Sherman's cannon roared, the solid shot streaking across the snow-covered ground. The tungsten round struck the Panther's rear armor with a deafening crack, punching through the engine compartment. Flames erupted from the hull, the fire spreading rapidly as fuel and ammunition ignited.

The Panther's turret swung erratically, its crew desperately trying to escape. The hatch opened, and two men scrambled out, their uniforms ablaze. One fell into the snow, his screams silenced as the fire consumed him. The other staggered a few steps before collapsing, his charred body motionless against the white ground.

"Target destroyed," Mike said, his voice cold.

"Good shot," Jack replied. "Quick Hands, reload. Grizzly, keep scanning."

The Iron Wolf moved cautiously past the burning wreckage, the flames crackling in the frozen air. The stench of burning fuel and flesh was overwhelming, mixing with the metallic tang of the cold.

"Another one down," Tom muttered, his breath visible as he spoke. "But there's always more."

"And we'll deal with them," Jack said firmly. "Stay sharp. This fight's not over."

The crew nodded, their resolve hardened despite the biting cold and the horrors they had just witnessed. The Iron Wolf pressed on, a lone predator in the frozen hell of the Ardennes, determined to survive the Battle of the Bulge.

The Iron Wolf sat in a defensive position at the edge of a clearing, its crew bracing against the bitter cold. Snowflakes fell steadily, blanketing the frozen ground in a pristine white that was quickly marred by the churn of boots and tracks. The platoon was cut off—no reinforcements, no resupply, and the radio chatter had gone disturbingly silent.

"Looks like it's just us out here," George "Grizzly" Thompson muttered, his eyes scanning the treeline through the bow gun sight. "The Krauts know it, too."

Jack "Boss" Harris adjusted his position in the turret, his breath visible in the frigid air. "Let them come. We hold this position, no matter what."

"Not much of a position," Tom "Wheels" Anderson said, his hands resting on the controls. "A clearing surrounded by trees? Feels like a setup for an ambush."

"It's what we've got," Jack replied. "Grizzly, keep that bow gun hot. Deadeye, be ready to fire. Quick Hands, shotgun round loaded?"

Joe "Quick Hands" Martinez nodded, his hands moving quickly despite the cold. "Shotgun's in the breech. Just say the word."

The forest was unnervingly silent, the snow muffling all sound. Then, faintly at first, came the crunch of boots on frozen ground. The sound grew louder, joined by guttural German commands echoing through the trees.

"They're coming," Mike "Deadeye" Walker said from his gunner's seat. "I see movement—lots of it."

Jack swung the periscope toward the treeline, his stomach tightening at the sight. Dozens of German infantry were advancing through the snow, their rifles and submachine guns raised. Some carried Panzerfausts, their rocket launchers poised to take out the Shermans.

"Infantry charge!" Jack shouted. "Grizzly, suppressing fire! Deadeye, hold until they're closer!"

George opened up with the bow gun, the .30-caliber rounds tearing into the advancing troops. Men dropped in the snow, their blood staining the white ground, but the Germans kept coming, their shouts growing louder as they neared the tanks.

"They're not stopping!" George yelled, his voice tight with adrenaline. "They're gonna swarm us!"

"Deadeye, shotgun round, center mass!" Jack ordered.

"On it!" Mike replied, swinging the turret toward the largest cluster of advancing soldiers. He took a deep breath, steadying his aim. "Firing!"

The 75mm cannon roared, firing the canister round directly into the oncoming charge. The shell exploded mid-air, releasing hundreds of steel balls in a deadly spread. The effect was instantaneous. The front ranks of the German charge were shredded, their bodies torn apart by the hail of projectiles. Blood sprayed across the snow, and the screams of the wounded filled the air as the remaining soldiers faltered.

"Reload!" Jack barked.

"Shotgun reloaded!" Joe called out, slamming another canister round into the breech.

"Grizzly, keep firing! Don't let them regroup!" Jack shouted.

George continued to rake the treeline with the bow gun, cutting down anyone who tried to move forward. The Germans hesitated, their momentum broken by the devastating firepower of the Iron Wolf and the other tanks in the platoon.

"They're pulling back!" Mike reported. "What's left of them, anyway."

Jack scanned the battlefield through his periscope. The snow was littered with bodies, mangled and broken from the shotgun round and machine-gun fire. The surviving Germans retreated into the trees, their shouts fading into the distance.

"Good work, everyone," Jack said, his voice steady. "But don't get comfortable. They'll be back."

The crew slumped slightly in their seats, the adrenaline fading and the cold creeping back into their bones. Outside, the snow continued to fall, covering the blood-soaked ground like a macabre shroud.

"That was close," Tom muttered, his breath visible in the freezing air. "Too close."

"It's gonna get worse," Jack replied grimly. "We're cut off, and they know it. This isn't over."

Inside the Iron Wolf, the crew steeled themselves for the next wave, knowing the fight was far from finished. The frozen hell of the Ardennes demanded everything they had, and the only way out was to keep fighting.

The Iron Wolf sat idle, its engine off to conserve fuel, the cold creeping into every crevice of the steel hull. Outside, the darkness was absolute, broken only by the faint glow of distant fires and the occasional flash of artillery on the horizon. The snow-covered forest seemed eerily still, but the crew knew better than to believe the quiet.

Inside the tank, the freezing air was stifling. Frost formed on the interior walls, and the crew's breaths came in visible puffs, each man bundled in whatever layers he could find. Despite their exhaustion, sleep was impossible.

Jack "Boss" Harris sat in the turret, his legs stiff from the cramped quarters. His gloved hands clutched the periscope, scanning the darkness for any sign of movement. "Deadeye, what do you see?" he asked quietly.

Mike "Deadeye" Walker shook his head, his voice low. "Nothing yet. But they're out there. I can feel it."

"Yeah," George "Grizzly" Thompson muttered from the bow gun. "You can hear them, too. Moving around, setting up. They're waiting for something."

"Probably for us to freeze to death," Tom "Wheels" Anderson muttered, rubbing his hands together in an attempt to stay warm. "Feels like my blood's turning to ice."

"Could be worse," Joe "Quick Hands" Martinez said, trying to muster some humor. "At least we're not out there in the snow."

"Yeah," George replied, "but at least out there, you can move around. Inside here? Feels like we're frozen in place."

Jack glanced around the cramped interior, his eyes settling on each member of his crew. Their faces were pale and drawn, their usual banter replaced by quiet tension. He sighed and leaned back against the turret ring. "We'll make it through this," he said firmly. "We've been through worse."

"Have we?" Mike asked, his tone skeptical. "North Africa was bad, sure. Normandy was hell. But this? This is different. It's the cold, the isolation... feels like we're just waiting to die."

"We're not dying here," Jack said sharply, his voice cutting through the gloom. "Not if we keep our heads. The Krauts are out there, sure, but they're cold and hungry too. They're just men, same as us."

The tank fell silent again, save for the faint sounds of distant movement outside. The occasional crack of a branch or muffled shout reached their ears, a reminder that the enemy was close.

"What do you think they're saying out there?" Joe asked after a while. "The Germans, I mean."

"Probably the same stuff we're saying," George replied. "How much they hate this place. How much they want to go home."

Tom shook his head. "Home feels like another life," he said softly. "Like it's not even real anymore."

"It's real," Jack said. "You just have to keep fighting for it."

"Easy for you to say," George muttered. "You're always the one telling us to hold it together. Don't you ever get scared, Boss?"

Jack hesitated, his gaze distant. "Of course I do," he admitted. "Every damn day. But fear keeps you alive. It keeps you sharp. Just don't let it take over."

The crew nodded, the unspoken bond between them growing stronger in the silence. They were scared, cold, and exhausted, but they were in it together. That meant something.

As the hours dragged on, the distant sounds of German movements continued, the occasional crackle of a radio or barked command carrying through the still night. The crew listened intently, their hands hovering over controls and weapons, ready for an attack that might never come.

Jack leaned back, closing his eyes for a moment. "Get what rest you can," he said softly. "We'll need it."

One by one, the crew settled into uneasy positions, their bodies stiff from the cold. The Iron Wolf stood like a silent sentinel in the darkness, its crew resolved to survive the night and whatever came next.

The Iron Wolf sat in the clearing, its hull dusted with frost and snow as dawn began to break. The faint gray light illuminated the battlefield, revealing the stark devastation around them. The crew inside the Sherman remained tense, their eyes heavy with exhaustion and their breaths visible in the freezing air.

Jack "Boss" Harris scanned the horizon through his periscope, searching for any sign of movement. The distant sounds of the German forces—the occasional shouted command, the clatter of equipment—had grown louder during the night. The enemy was preparing for another assault, and the Iron Wolf was in no condition for another prolonged fight.

"Boss, you hear that?" George "Grizzly" Thompson asked from the bow gun, his voice tense. "They're gearing up. Won't be long now."

Jack nodded, his jaw tightening. "Stay sharp, Grizz. Deadeye, what's the status on the main gun?"

"Loaded and ready," Mike "Deadeye" Walker replied, his hands steady on the controls. "Just waiting for the first poor bastard to pop his head up."

"Quick Hands, keep us stocked," Jack ordered. "Wheels, if we need to move, keep it slow and steady. No slipping on this ice."

"Got it, Boss," Tom "Wheels" Anderson said, his voice weary but focused.

The minutes stretched on, the tension inside the tank thick enough to cut with a knife. Then, in the distance, the unmistakable sound of aircraft engines broke through the silence. The low, throaty roar of Allied fighters approaching from the west sent a wave of relief through the crew.

"Air support!" Joe "Quick Hands" Martinez exclaimed, a rare smile crossing his face. "They're finally here!"

Jack shifted the periscope, catching sight of the sleek shapes of P-47 Thunderbolts swooping low over the treetops. The planes unleashed a hail of rockets and machine-gun fire, tearing into the German positions with devastating precision. Explosions rocked the forest as bunkers and vehicles were obliterated, sending plumes of smoke and debris into the air.

"Looks like they're hitting the Krauts hard," Mike said, his voice tinged with hope.

"And about damn time," George muttered, his hands relaxing slightly on the bow gun.

The radio crackled with a new transmission. "All units, this is Command. Reinforcements have arrived. Infantry and armor are advancing on your position. Hold tight and prepare to regroup."

Jack keyed the mic. "Iron Wolf copies. Holding position."

Moments later, the rumble of Allied tanks and trucks echoed through the clearing. Fresh Sherman tanks rolled into view, their crews waving as they joined the line. Infantry poured out of half-tracks, their rifles raised as they swept through the area to secure it.

"We're not alone anymore," Tom said, his voice filled with relief.

Jack climbed out of the turret, the cold air biting at his face as he stood on the hull. He raised a hand to one of the approaching tank commanders, who returned the gesture with a nod.

"Looks like reinforcements are here to save the day," Jack said, his voice carrying into the tank. "We made it."

The crew began to relax, the weight of the night's tension easing as the fresh troops moved in to relieve them. Medics tended to the wounded, and mechanics began inspecting the battered tanks for repairs.

As the sun rose higher, the battlefield took on an almost surreal quality. The smoke from the airstrikes mixed with the crisp morning air, and the snow glistened under the pale light. The horrors of the night were still fresh, but for the first time in days, there was a sense of hope.

"Boss," George called from the bow gun. "Think this means we get a break?"

Jack smirked faintly, climbing back into the turret. "Not likely, Grizz. But at least we've got backup now."

The Iron Wolf roared back to life, its engine shaking off the cold as the crew prepared to move out. The reinforcements had arrived, but the Battle of the Bulge was far from over. For now, though, the crew of the Iron Wolf had earned a moment to regroup, to breathe, and to

prepare for the next fight.

Chapter 10: Pushing Back

The Iron Wolf roared forward with the rest of the tank company, its tracks crunching through snow and ice as it led the charge to reclaim the territory lost during the German offensive. Allied forces were no longer on the defensive; this was a counteroffensive, and the crew of the Sherman felt the shift in momentum as they surged across the frozen ground.

"Feels good to be on the attack for once," George "Grizzly" Thompson muttered, his hands steady on the bow gun controls. "Tired of waiting around to get hit."

"Just don't get cocky," Jack "Boss" Harris warned from the turret. "The Germans aren't giving this up without a fight."

The radio crackled with updates from the column. "All units, advance with caution. Enemy positions may be fortified. Expect resistance."

Jack keyed the mic. "Iron Wolf copies. Moving up."

The battlefield ahead was a patchwork of craters, shattered trees, and frozen corpses. The German Nebelwerfer batteries—deadly rocket launchers known as "Screaming Meemies"—had torn through Allied positions during the initial offensive, leaving a trail of destruction. Now, the tank company was tasked with destroying those batteries and breaking the enemy's grip on the area.

"Boss, you see that?" Mike "Deadeye" Walker asked, adjusting the gun sight. "Looks like smoke trails up ahead. Could be Nebelwerfers."

Jack peered through his periscope, spotting faint plumes of smoke rising from a treeline in the distance. "Deadeye's right. That's where they're firing from. Wheels, take us left, into the cover of those trees. Quick Hands, load a Boomer."

"Boomer loaded," Joe "Quick Hands" Martinez called out, his hands steady despite the tension.

The Iron Wolf veered into the treeline, its engine rumbling as it approached the suspected position. The rest of the tank company followed, their turrets swiveling to cover all angles. The distant sound of rockets launching echoed across the battlefield, a high-pitched wail that sent a chill down everyone's spine.

"There they are," Jack said, his voice low. Through the trees, he could see the Nebelwerfer battery—a cluster of rocket launchers set up in a clearing, their crews hurriedly reloading for another salvo.

"Deadeye, target the center launcher," Jack ordered. "Grizzly, cover the flanks. We don't want any infantry sneaking up on us."

"On target," Mike replied, his hands steady on the gun controls. "Firing."

The Sherman's cannon roared, sending a high-explosive shell streaking toward the battery. The round struck the center launcher, detonating with a deafening explosion. The force of the blast tore the Nebelwerfer apart, scattering its crew like rag dolls. Body parts and twisted metal rained down, staining the snow with blood and debris.

"Direct hit!" Mike called out, already lining up another shot.

"Quick Hands, reload!" Jack barked.

"Boomer reloaded!" Joe replied, slamming the shell into the breech.

"Deadeye, take out the next launcher," Jack commanded.

Mike fired again, the shell striking another Nebelwerfer and igniting the rockets still loaded in its tubes. The resulting explosion was catastrophic, a fireball that engulfed the nearby crew and sent shards of metal flying through the air. The screams of the dying were audible even inside the tank.

"Christ," George muttered, his voice shaking slightly. "That's a hell of a way to go."

"They didn't give our guys any mercy," Jack said coldly. "Now they're getting a taste of their own medicine."

The remaining Nebelwerfers were abandoned as their crews fled, leaving the burning launchers behind. Allied infantry swept into the area, finishing off any stragglers and securing the position.

"All units, the battery is neutralized," came the voice of Lieutenant Parker over the radio. "Good work. Continue advancing and clear out any remaining resistance."

Jack exhaled, his grip on the turret ring loosening slightly. "Wheels, move us forward. Grizzly, keep an eye out for ambushes. Deadeye, stay ready."

The Iron Wolf rolled into the smoldering clearing, the crew grimly taking in the devastation they had wrought. The Nebelwerfer battery was nothing more than a collection of charred wreckage and mangled bodies, a stark reminder of the brutality of war.

"Think they'll fire on us again?" Joe asked quietly.

"Not from here, they won't," Mike replied, his voice hard.

Jack nodded, his gaze fixed on the horizon. "We keep pushing. Every step forward is one closer to ending this."

The Iron Wolf pressed on, leading the charge to retake lost ground. The Germans had been dealt a crippling blow, but the crew knew the fight was far from over. For now, though, they had the upper hand—and they intended to keep it.

The Iron Wolf crawled through the ruined landscape, its tracks grinding over snow and frozen dirt. Smoke hung low over the battlefield, mingling with the sharp scent of cordite and the coppery tang of blood. The counteroffensive was taking its toll on both sides, and every inch of ground was paid for in lives.

Inside the tank, the crew was silent, the weight of the past hours pressing down on them. Skirmish after skirmish had left their nerves frayed and their bodies weary, but the enemy kept coming.

"All units, hold your positions," the radio crackled with Lieutenant Parker's strained voice. "We've got reports of another German counterattack. Tanks and infantry. Be ready."

Jack "Boss" Harris nodded grimly, his eyes fixed on the periscope. "You heard him. Deadeye, stay on the gun. Grizzly, keep that bow gun scanning. Wheels, we'll need to move if they get too close."

"Boss," Joe "Quick Hands" Martinez said softly from his position near the ammo rack. "You think this ends anytime soon? Feels like we're just bleeding each other dry out here."

Jack didn't answer immediately. He knew the truth—the Battle of the Bulge was a grinding war of attrition, and no one would leave this frozen wasteland unchanged.

Before he could respond, the sharp crack of a German 75mm cannon echoed across the battlefield. Jack swung the periscope toward the source, spotting a Panzer IV advancing through the haze. Its turret fired again, the shell streaking past the Iron Wolf and slamming into a Sherman in their column.

The hit was devastating. The tank shuddered under the impact, its armor crumpling as flames erupted from the engine compartment. Joe watched in horror as the commander—a man named Charlie, whom he'd shared rations and stories with just days before—scrambled to escape the turret. He barely made it halfway out before a secondary explosion engulfed the tank, throwing his lifeless body into the snow.

"Charlie!" Joe shouted, his voice cracking as he lunged toward the side hatch, instinctively trying to get out.

Jack grabbed his arm, pulling him back. "Stay inside, Joe! There's nothing you can do!"

Joe's face twisted in anguish, his hands trembling as he stared out the viewport at the burning wreckage. "He didn't even have a chance…" he whispered.

"None of us do if we don't keep it together," Jack said sharply. "We'll make them pay for it, but right now, we survive. Do you hear me?"

Joe nodded reluctantly, his eyes still fixed on the flames as tears froze on his cheeks. "Yeah… I hear you."

"Deadeye, target that Panzer!" Jack barked, his voice snapping the crew back to focus. "Quick Hands, load solid shot!"

"Solid shot loaded!" Joe called, his hands moving automatically.

Mike "Deadeye" Walker swung the turret, locking onto the Panzer IV as it lined up another shot. "On target," he said through gritted teeth. "Firing!"

The Iron Wolf's cannon roared, the tungsten-core round streaking through the smoke and slamming into the Panzer's side armor. The German tank erupted in a fireball, its turret ripping free and landing several feet away. The crew didn't make it out.

"Target destroyed," Mike said coldly, already scanning for the next threat.

"Good shot," Jack said. "Grizzly, cover the infantry. Wheels, move us forward."

The Iron Wolf advanced cautiously, its bow gun spitting bullets to suppress the scattered German infantry. Around them, the battlefield was chaos. Soldiers screamed and shouted, tanks burned, and the snow was churned into a bloody mess beneath the tracks of advancing vehicles.

Inside the tank, the silence was heavy, each man processing the loss of their comrades in their own way. Joe sat against the ammo rack, his hands trembling as he loaded the next shell. He didn't speak, but the pain in his eyes was unmistakable.

"Charlie was a good man," Tom "Wheels" Anderson said quietly, his voice breaking the silence. "We'll make sure his death wasn't for nothing."

"None of this is for nothing," Jack said firmly, though his own doubts lingered in the back of his mind. "We keep fighting. We keep moving. That's how we honor them."

The crew nodded, their resolve hardened but their hearts heavier than ever. The Iron Wolf pressed on, leading the charge through the frozen hell of the Ardennes. The war of attrition continued, and the cost of every victory grew higher with each passing hour.

The Iron Wolf moved cautiously through the snowy terrain, its turret swiveling back and forth as the crew scanned for threats. Smoke from burning tanks and vehicles hung heavy in the air, mingling with the sharp chill of the Ardennes winter. Every step forward felt like a gamble—one wrong move, and they'd face the devastating firepower of another enemy ambush.

Jack "Boss" Harris peered through the periscope, his grip tightening as he spotted movement in the distance. "Hold up, Wheels," he said sharply. "Deadeye, what do you see? Eleven o'clock."

Mike "Deadeye" Walker adjusted the gun sight, his face grim as he focused on the shape coming into view. "Panther," he said, his voice low but steady. "Half-hidden by those trees, but it's definitely a Panther."

The Panther sat in a slight depression, its angular hull blending into the snowy backdrop. Its long 75mm gun was scanning for targets, its crew clearly on high alert. Jack knew they wouldn't get a second chance if the German tank spotted them first.

"Wheels, back us into cover," Jack ordered. "Deadeye, keep your sights on it but don't fire yet. Grizzly, watch the flanks—there could be infantry covering it. Quick Hands, load solid shot."

"Solid shot loaded," Joe "Quick Hands" Martinez replied, his hands moving quickly despite the tension in the air.

Tom "Wheels" Anderson reversed the Iron Wolf into the cover of a fallen tree, its thick branches providing a sliver of concealment. The crew sat in tense silence, the only sound the faint hum of the tank's engine and the distant crack of gunfire.

"Alright," Jack said, his voice calm but firm. "Here's the plan. We're not winning a straight-up fight with that thing. Wheels, take us wide left. We'll flank it and get a shot at its side. Deadeye, be ready to fire as soon as we've got the angle."

"Got it," Mike said, his hands steady on the gun controls.

"Let's hope it doesn't see us first," George "Grizzly" Thompson muttered, his bow gun swiveling to cover their advance.

The Iron Wolf moved slowly, its tracks crunching through the snow as it circled around the Panther's position. The German tank remained stationary, its turret scanning the opposite direction, unaware of the Sherman's maneuver.

"Almost there," Jack whispered, his eyes fixed on the Panther. "Wheels, hold steady. Deadeye, you've got the shot. Aim for the side, just below the turret."

Mike adjusted the sights, his finger hovering over the trigger. "On target," he said. "Firing!"

The 75mm cannon roared, the solid shot streaking across the battlefield and slamming into the Panther's side armor. The round punched through with a deafening crack, hitting the engine compartment. Flames erupted from the rear of the German tank, smoke pouring from the vents as the crew inside scrambled to escape.

The Panther's turret began to swing toward the Iron Wolf, but it was too late. The damage was done. One by one, the German crew bailed out, their figures silhouetted against the flames as they jumped into the snow.

"Grizzly, take them out!" Jack ordered.

George didn't hesitate. The bow gun opened up, spitting .30-caliber rounds at the escaping crew. The machine-gun fire cut through the snow, catching the first man in the chest and sending him tumbling backward. The second man ran a few steps before falling face-first into the snow, blood staining the pristine white.

The remaining two crew members hesitated, one holding his hands up in surrender. George hesitated, his finger hovering over the trigger.

"Hold fire," Jack said sharply. "We've done enough."

The two surviving crew members collapsed to their knees, their hands raised as Allied infantry swarmed the area, taking them prisoner. The Panther burned behind them, its flames crackling in the cold air.

"Target neutralized," Mike said, his voice steady but tinged with exhaustion.

"Good work," Jack replied, his tone firm. "Quick Hands, reload. Wheels, move us forward. Grizzly, keep watching those flanks."

The Iron Wolf pressed on, leaving the smoldering wreckage of the Panther behind. The duel had been tense, but the crew's tactics had prevailed. Inside the tank, the men shared a brief moment of relief, knowing they had survived another close call. The battle raged on, and the Iron Wolf was determined to see it through.

The Iron Wolf rolled to a halt at the edge of a ridge, its engine idling as the crew took in the scene below. The once-battered Allied forces were advancing in full force, their tanks and infantry pushing through the remnants of the German lines. Smoke rose from burning vehicles, and the distant sound of gunfire was fading as the German offensive began to crumble.

Jack "Boss" Harris peered through his periscope, scanning the battlefield. "Looks like they're pulling back," he said, his voice tinged with cautious relief. "The Krauts are done here."

"About damn time," George "Grizzly" Thompson muttered, slumping back in his seat at the bow gun. "I was starting to think this fight would never end."

Mike "Deadeye" Walker adjusted his position at the gunner's seat, his eyes fixed on the distant horizon. "They threw everything they had at us," he said. "And we're still standing."

"Barely," Joe "Quick Hands" Martinez replied, leaning against the ammo rack. "We've been lucky. A lot of guys out there weren't."

The radio crackled to life, bringing a message from Lieutenant Parker. "All units, the German offensive has collapsed. Reinforcements are securing the area. Hold your position and prepare to regroup. Good work, everyone."

Jack exhaled, the tension in his shoulders easing slightly. "You heard him," he said to the crew. "We did it. The Bulge is ours."

The Iron Wolf's crew allowed themselves a moment of relief, their exhaustion palpable after days of relentless combat. The tank had been their shield, their weapon, and their home through the bitter fighting, and it had carried them through one of the toughest battles of the war.

Tom "Wheels" Anderson leaned back in his seat, his hands still on the controls. "So what now?" he asked, his voice weary but hopeful. "Do we finally get a break?"

Jack shook his head. "Not likely. The war's still on. This is just one victory in a long list of fights we've got ahead of us."

"Yeah," George said, his voice soft. "But it's a big one. Feels like we've turned the tide, you know?"

Mike nodded, his expression unreadable. "It's a step forward. But don't get comfortable. The Krauts aren't done fighting yet."

Joe, who had been silent for most of the morning, finally spoke. "Charlie would've liked this," he said quietly, his eyes fixed on the snow-covered battlefield. "Seeing us push them back. He'd have been proud."

Jack glanced at him, his voice steady. "Charlie would be proud of all of us. We've fought like hell to get here, and we're not stopping now."

The crew nodded, a sense of camaraderie settling over them as they shared a moment of quiet reflection. Outside, the battlefield was slowly transforming. Allied soldiers moved through the wreckage, securing prisoners and clearing debris. Medics tended to the wounded, and engineers worked to repair the battered tanks and vehicles.

As the Iron Wolf sat motionless, its engine rumbling softly, Jack allowed himself a rare smile. "Grizzly, you still got that lucky coin?"

George pulled the battered coin from his pocket, holding it up for the crew to see. "Still here," he said with a grin. "And it's not going anywhere."

"Good," Jack replied. "Keep it close. We're going to need all the luck we can get."

The crew chuckled softly, the tension of the past days easing slightly as they allowed themselves a brief moment of levity. The Battle of the Bulge was over, but the war was far from won. For now, though, they had a victory to hold onto, and the Iron Wolf would be ready for whatever came next.

As the tank idled on the ridge, the crew looked out over the battlefield, their faces a mix of exhaustion and determination. They had survived the frozen hell of the Ardennes, and they would keep pushing forward until the war was finally over.

The Iron Wolf rumbled through the snow-covered fields, the frozen terrain giving way to patches of churned earth as the tank company advanced. The Battle of the Bulge was behind them, but the war was far from over. Orders had come down from command: the Allied forces were to push into Germany, crossing the Rhine and breaking the final resistance of the German war machine.

Jack "Boss" Harris leaned against the turret ring, his eyes fixed on the horizon through the periscope. The snow was starting to melt, turning the ground into a cold, slushy mess. The once-quiet fields were now teeming with activity as tanks, trucks, and infantry assembled for the next phase of the campaign.

"Feels strange," George "Grizzly" Thompson said from the bow gun. "Pushing into Germany. Feels like we're stepping into the lion's den."

"Better than getting pushed back again," Mike "Deadeye" Walker replied, adjusting the gun sights. "We've got momentum now. Let's keep it."

"Still doesn't feel real," Joe "Quick Hands" Martinez said softly, his voice carrying the weight of exhaustion. "We've been fighting for so long… pushing into their territory makes it feel like maybe, just maybe, this is the beginning of the end."

Tom "Wheels" Anderson let out a humorless chuckle as he tightened a bolt on the driver's controls. "Don't get too excited, Quick Hands. Something tells me the Krauts aren't gonna roll over and let us walk in."

Jack keyed the radio, listening to the chatter from command. Orders were coming in steadily: formations were being arranged, supply lines fortified, and artillery prepared for the final push across the Rhine. The scope of the operation was enormous, but Jack knew every tank and crew would play their part.

"All units, be advised," came the familiar voice of Lieutenant Parker over the radio. "We're moving out at first light. Make sure your vehicles are prepped and your crews are rested. This is it, boys. We're taking the fight to their doorstep."

Jack switched off the radio and turned to his crew. "You heard him. Wheels, check the tracks and engine one more time. Grizzly, inspect the bow gun. Deadeye, make sure the cannon's ready to fire. Quick Hands, stock us up with whatever ammo you can get your hands on."

"On it, Boss," the crew replied in unison, their weariness momentarily overridden by the urgency of the task ahead.

As the crew went about their duties, the camp buzzed with activity. Mechanics worked on repairing damaged tanks, their tools clanking against steel. Medics tended to the wounded, and supply officers distributed rations and ammunition to the men. The mood was tense but determined.

Jack stepped outside the Sherman for a moment, the cold air biting at his face. He looked out over the makeshift staging area, taking in the sight of the gathered forces. This was more than just a battle—it was the beginning of the endgame. The thought both exhilarated and terrified him.

George climbed out of the tank and joined Jack, flipping his lucky coin in the air. "What do you think, Boss?" he asked. "We make it through this?"

Jack watched the coin spin, catching the faint glint of sunlight reflecting off its worn surface. "We've made it this far," he said finally. "And we'll keep making it. One step at a time."

George caught the coin and pocketed it with a grin. "Good enough for me."

The crew reconvened inside the tank as night fell, their preparations complete. They ate their meager rations in silence, the anticipation of the next day hanging over them like a weight.

As they settled in for a restless night, Jack addressed them one last time. "This isn't just another battle. We're crossing into Germany. This is their turf, and they're going to fight like hell to keep us out. But we've been through worse, and we'll get through this too. Stay sharp, watch each other's backs, and don't lose focus."

The crew nodded, their faces a mix of exhaustion and determination. They knew the road ahead would be brutal, but they also knew they had each other—and the Iron Wolf.

As the first light of dawn broke over the camp, the engines of the tank company roared to life. The Iron Wolf led the column forward, its tracks carving a path through the snow and mud. The final push had begun, and the crew braced themselves for the fight of their lives.

Chapter 11: Crossing the Rhine

The Iron Wolf rolled into position near the edge of the Rhine, its turret scanning the horizon as the crew prepared for the monumental operation ahead. The river loomed before them, wide and fast-moving, its icy waters reflecting the faint light of dawn. The German forces had fortified the opposite bank, their artillery and machine guns poised to repel any attempt to cross.

"All units, this is Command," the radio crackled. "Prepare to support the crossing. Artillery is targeting key positions on the far side, but resistance is expected to be heavy. Tanks will provide cover for the engineers and infantry. Be ready for anything."

Jack "Boss" Harris adjusted his periscope, scanning the distant treeline on the opposite bank. "Grizzly, keep that bow gun hot. Deadeye, be ready to fire at anything that moves. Quick Hands, load a Boomer. Wheels, stand by to reposition on my mark."

"Boomer loaded," Joe "Quick Hands" Martinez confirmed, his hands steady despite the tension.

The sound of Allied artillery began to fill the air, the deep thud of the guns shaking the ground beneath them. Shells streaked through the sky, exploding along the German-held bank in massive plumes of dirt and debris. Jack watched as entire sections of the treeline disappeared in the chaos, but the return fire from the Germans was immediate and deadly.

"Here they go," George "Grizzly" Thompson muttered, his eyes fixed on the opposite bank. "They're not gonna make this easy."

German artillery roared back, shells landing dangerously close to the Allied staging area. The Iron Wolf shuddered as a blast hit nearby, showering the tank with dirt and rocks.

"Boss, we've got movement!" Mike "Deadeye" Walker called out. "Bunker at one o'clock, just above the riverbank. Looks like they're targeting our engineers."

Jack focused on the bunker through his periscope. The fortified position was built into the hillside, its camouflaged roof partially hidden by the treeline. Muzzle flashes from its machine guns tore through the dawn light, pinning down the Allied infantry attempting to move closer to the river.

"Deadeye, take it out!" Jack barked. "Quick Hands, be ready with another Boomer."

"On target," Mike said, his voice calm and steady. He fired, the Sherman's cannon roaring as the high-explosive shell streaked toward the bunker.

The round hit dead center, detonating with a thunderous explosion. The roof of the bunker collapsed inward, sending a cloud of dirt and concrete shards into the air. German soldiers were thrown from the structure, their bodies cartwheeling through the sky before landing lifeless on the ground below. The wreckage burned, thick black smoke rising into the cold air.

"Direct hit," Mike reported, already scanning for another target.

"Good shot," Jack said, his voice sharp. "Grizzly, keep an eye on the flanks. Quick Hands, reload."

"Boomer reloaded," Joe replied, sliding another shell into the breech.

The Iron Wolf pushed forward, its tracks churning through the muddy ground as it provided cover for the engineers setting up pontoon bridges across the river. The Germans continued to fire, their artillery and machine guns focusing on the crossing points.

"Wheels, move us to that ridge," Jack ordered. "We'll have a better angle on their positions."

Tom "Wheels" Anderson guided the Sherman up a slight incline, the tank's engine straining against the weight and slippery terrain. From their new vantage point, the crew could see the chaos unfolding along the riverbank. Allied infantry were pinned down, taking heavy fire as they tried to secure the bridgehead.

"Deadeye, another bunker, eleven o'clock!" Jack called out.

Mike swung the turret, lining up the shot. The German position was pouring fire onto the advancing infantry, but the Iron Wolf's cannon roared again, silencing it with another devastating explosion.

"Bunker neutralized," Mike said grimly. "But there's still a lot of heat coming from the treeline."

"We keep hitting them," Jack replied. "Every shot we take is one less firing at our boys."

As the battle raged on, the Allied forces began to make headway. The engineers completed the first pontoon bridge, and infantry began crossing under the cover of tank fire. The Iron Wolf continued to pound the German positions, its cannon delivering deadly precision that cleared the way for the advancing troops.

Inside the tank, the crew was tense but focused, their movements precise as they reloaded, aimed, and fired with practiced efficiency. The crossing of the Rhine was underway, and the Iron Wolf was at the forefront of the fight, leading the charge into the heart of Germany.

The Iron Wolf rolled into the outskirts of a small German town, its engine rumbling softly as the crew scanned the narrow streets for threats. The cobblestone roads and tightly packed buildings made movement slow and treacherous, every corner a potential ambush. The town had been abandoned by civilians, leaving only German defenders entrenched in its ruins.

"Deadeye, keep that cannon ready," Jack "Boss" Harris ordered, his eyes scanning the twisting streets through the periscope. "Grizzly, watch the windows. Quick Hands, load a Boomer. Wheels, take it slow—no sudden turns."

"Boomer loaded," Joe "Quick Hands" Martinez replied, sliding the high-explosive shell into the breech.

"Feels like we're crawling into a trap," George "Grizzly" Thompson muttered from the bow gun. "I don't like it."

"None of us do," Jack replied. "Stay sharp."

The Sherman crept forward, its tracks grinding against the cobblestones. Allied infantry followed closely behind, their rifles raised as they scanned the windows and doorways for signs of movement. The town was eerily quiet, the only sounds the faint whistle of wind and the distant rumble of artillery.

Then, without warning, a rifle shot cracked through the air, followed by a hail of machine-gun fire. The infantry dove for cover, shouting warnings as bullets ricocheted off the tank's hull.

"Snipers!" one of the soldiers shouted. "Third floor, red building!"

Jack swung the periscope toward the source of the fire, spotting the muzzle flashes coming from a crumbling three-story building. "Deadeye, third floor of that red building," he barked. "Grizzly, lay down suppressing fire on the lower windows."

"Got it!" George shouted, the bow gun roaring to life as he sprayed the building's facade.

Mike "Deadeye" Walker lined up the shot, his hands steady on the gun controls. "On target," he said. "Firing!"

The Sherman's cannon roared, the high-explosive shell slamming into the third floor. The blast tore through the building, sending debris flying into the street. The machine-gun fire ceased, but as the dust settled, more rifle shots rang out from the lower floors.

"They're still in there!" Jack shouted. "Quick Hands, load another Boomer! Wheels, move us into a better angle."

"Boomer reloaded," Joe called, his voice tense but controlled.

Tom "Wheels" Anderson guided the tank into position, its tracks grinding over rubble as the Iron Wolf angled for a clear shot at the building's foundation.

"Deadeye, hit the base of the building," Jack ordered. "Bring the whole thing down."

Mike nodded, his face grim as he adjusted the turret. "On target," he said. "Firing!"

The cannon roared again, the shell striking the base of the building with devastating force. The explosion shook the ground, and the structure groaned loudly before collapsing in on itself. Bricks, wood, and steel beams tumbled into the street, burying the defenders under tons of rubble.

The street fell silent, the only sounds the crackling of fires and the distant echoes of gunfire from other parts of the town.

"Target neutralized," Mike said coldly, his eyes fixed on the smoldering pile of debris.

"Good work," Jack replied. "Grizzly, keep scanning for movement. Quick Hands, reload. Wheels, hold position for now."

The infantry moved up cautiously, checking the rubble for any surviving defenders. One of the soldiers signaled back to the tank, giving a thumbs-up to indicate the threat was eliminated.

Inside the Iron Wolf, the crew took a moment to catch their breath. The cramped interior was filled with the acrid smell of gunpowder and sweat, their nerves frayed from the close-quarters combat.

"Urban fighting," George muttered, shaking his head. "Every damn building's a death trap."

"Welcome to the final push," Jack said grimly. "It's only going to get worse from here."

The Sherman pressed forward, navigating the narrow streets as the crew braced themselves for the next ambush. The town was just the beginning—a small piece of the larger battle to break the German defenses and secure the path to victory. Inside the Iron Wolf, the crew remained vigilant, knowing the fight was far from over.

The Iron Wolf rumbled cautiously through the narrow streets of the German town, its crew on edge. The destruction of the sniper-held building had given the Allies a foothold, but the Germans weren't retreating quietly. Every shadow, every corner, seemed to promise danger.

"Stay sharp," Jack "Boss" Harris said over the intercom. "Grizzly, keep that bow gun ready. Wheels, slow it down—don't give them an opening. Deadeye, eyes on those upper floors."

"Got it, Boss," Tom "Wheels" Anderson replied, easing the tank forward.

The Sherman's engine growled softly, its tracks clanking over shattered cobblestones. Smoke and dust filled the air, mingling with the distant sound of gunfire and the crackle of flames. Allied infantry followed behind, using the tank as cover as they swept the streets.

Then, chaos erupted.

A sudden explosion rocked the tank, sending chunks of stone and dirt flying into the air. The Iron Wolf shuddered under the force of a Panzerfaust rocket hitting the side of the street, narrowly missing its hull. From the windows above, German infantry opened fire with rifles and machine guns, the bullets pinging off the Sherman's armor.

"Ambush!" George "Grizzly" Thompson shouted, swinging the bow gun toward the nearest source of fire. "They're everywhere!"

"Grizzly, light them up!" Jack barked. "Deadeye, scan for targets! Quick Hands, load a Willie Pete—we need smoke!"

The bow-mounted machine gun roared to life, spitting .30-caliber rounds into the windows and doorways. German soldiers fell back under the onslaught, some collapsing where they stood, their bodies slumping against shattered glass and splintered wood.

"Smoke round loaded!" Joe "Quick Hands" Martinez called out, his voice tight with adrenaline.

"Deadeye, fire at that alley!" Jack ordered. "Flush them out!"

Mike "Deadeye" Walker swiveled the turret, aiming at a narrow alley where German soldiers were firing from cover. He pulled the trigger, and the 75mm cannon roared, sending a white phosphorus round streaking into the confined space. The resulting explosion filled the alley with thick, choking smoke, forcing the defenders to flee—or burn.

"They're falling back!" Mike reported, his voice cold.

"Not all of them," George muttered, his finger on the trigger. "Here they come!"

From a side street, a squad of German infantry charged, shouting as they sprinted toward the Sherman with grenades and rifles. The bow gun roared again, cutting through the advancing soldiers with brutal efficiency. Bullets tore into flesh, spraying the cobblestones with blood. One man fell clutching his stomach, another dropping his rifle as he collapsed face-first into the snow.

"They just keep coming!" George yelled, the bow gun rattling under his grip.

"Keep firing!" Jack ordered. "Wheels, pivot us—don't let them flank!"

The Sherman's tracks ground against the cobblestones as Tom maneuvered the tank, keeping its front armor facing the attackers. The bow gun mowed down the last of the charging infantry, their bodies crumpling in the street.

"Clear for now," George said, his voice shaky. "But damn, that was close."

Jack scanned the area through his periscope. The street was littered with bodies, the snow stained red with blood and dotted with the twisted remains of rifles and grenades. Smoke hung in the air, mingling with the acrid stench of burning wood and gunpowder.

"Good work, everyone," Jack said, his tone steady. "But we're not out of this yet. Deadeye, keep scanning for threats. Quick Hands, reload. Wheels, stay ready to move."

"Boomer reloaded," Joe said, sliding another shell into the breech.

As the tank settled into a defensive position, the infantry behind it regrouped, their faces pale but determined. The ambush had been brutal, but the Iron Wolf had held its ground, its crew proving once again why they were at the forefront of the fight.

Inside the tank, the men shared a brief moment of relief, their breaths visible in the cold air. The ambush was over, but the fight for the town continued, and the crew of the Iron Wolf knew they'd face more danger before the day was done.

The Iron Wolf crept forward, its engine rumbling softly as the tank moved deeper into the heart of the German town. Allied infantry advanced alongside it, their weapons raised as they checked every doorway, window, and alley for signs of resistance. The town's defenders had been scattered by the earlier engagements, but pockets of determined German troops still held key positions.

"All units, listen up," the radio crackled with Lieutenant Parker's voice. "We need this town cleared by nightfall. Tanks, support the infantry. Watch for ambushes and civilian movement. Keep it clean."

Jack "Boss" Harris keyed the mic. "Iron Wolf copies. We're advancing."

The Sherman rolled cautiously through a narrow street, its turret swiveling as Mike "Deadeye" Walker scanned for targets. George "Grizzly" Thompson kept the bow gun ready, his eyes darting between the buildings. The tension was palpable, the crew knowing the next shot could come from anywhere.

"Grizzly, see anything?" Jack asked.

"Nothing yet," George replied. "But it's too quiet. You know how that goes."

Ahead, the infantry signaled for the tank to hold as they moved to clear a large stone building. Rifle shots rang out from the upper windows, and the soldiers ducked into cover, returning fire.

"Boss, movement on the left," Mike called out. "Second floor, red shutters."

Jack swung the periscope toward the building, catching a glimpse of a German machine gun firing from the second-floor window. "Deadeye, take it out. Quick Hands, load a Boomer."

"Boomer loaded," Joe "Quick Hands" Martinez replied.

"Firing!" Mike called, pulling the trigger.

The 75mm cannon roared, the high-explosive round slamming into the second floor. The explosion obliterated the machine gun position, the force of the blast sending debris and bodies flying. Smoke poured from the shattered window as the firing ceased.

"Target neutralized," Mike said coldly, already scanning for the next threat.

The infantry surged forward, clearing the building as the Iron Wolf advanced to cover them. The tank rolled past a row of houses, their windows dark and lifeless. Jack's periscope swept the area, every shadow a potential hiding spot.

Then, chaos erupted again.

A burst of machine-gun fire cracked through the air, this time from the upper floor of a civilian home. The rounds tore into the street, forcing the infantry to dive for cover. Jack cursed under his breath, quickly locating the source of the fire.

"Deadeye, that house—first window, top floor!" he shouted.

"On it," Mike replied, adjusting the turret.

"Boss, that's a civilian home!" George warned, his voice filled with hesitation.

"They're using it as a firing position," Jack said grimly. "We don't have a choice. Deadeye, fire."

The cannon roared again, the shell slamming into the upper floor of the house. The explosion ripped through the structure, sending shards of wood and stone raining down onto the street. The machine-gun fire stopped, but as the smoke cleared, the damage became painfully clear.

The upper floor of the house was gone, and flames licked at the edges of the shattered walls. From the rubble, a woman stumbled out, clutching a small child to her chest. Her face was streaked with ash and tears as she screamed, her cries cutting through the noise of battle.

"Jesus Christ," Joe whispered, his voice trembling. "There were civilians in there…"

Jack's stomach tightened, his hands gripping the turret ring. "We didn't know," he said, his voice hollow. "We couldn't know."

The infantry moved quickly, pulling the woman and child away from the burning building as medics rushed to help. The crew of the Iron Wolf sat in stunned silence, the weight of what had just happened pressing down on them.

"Boss…" George started, his voice breaking. "What the hell are we doing out here?"

Jack took a deep breath, forcing himself to focus. "We're fighting a war," he said quietly. "And sometimes… this is what it looks like. But we finish the mission. That's all we can do."

The tank pressed on, the crew shaken but determined to see the fight through. The streets grew quieter as the remaining pockets of resistance were cleared, but the memory of the burning house lingered in their minds. For the men of the Iron Wolf, victory came at a cost—and not all of it was paid by soldiers.

The Iron Wolf idled in the center of the shattered German town, its engine rumbling softly. Around it, Allied forces regrouped, their faces etched with exhaustion but their resolve unshaken. Smoke still hung heavy in the air, the remnants of destroyed buildings and vehicles casting long shadows in the fading light. The town was theirs, but the war was far from over.

Jack "Boss" Harris leaned against the turret, his helmet pushed back slightly as he listened to the distant hum of supply trucks rolling in. The crew inside the tank was quiet, the weight of the day's events pressing down on them like the cold night air.

The radio crackled, breaking the silence. "All units, be advised," came Lieutenant Parker's voice. "Orders just came down from command. We're advancing deeper into Germany. Expect increased resistance. Tanks and infantry will spearhead the push. Be ready to move at dawn."

Jack keyed the mic. "Iron Wolf copies. We'll be ready."

George "Grizzly" Thompson let out a low whistle from the bow gun. "Deeper into Germany, huh? Guess they're not letting us catch our breath."

"Wouldn't expect them to," Mike "Deadeye" Walker said, his voice flat. "The closer we get to their heart, the harder they'll fight."

"That's if we survive the trip," Joe "Quick Hands" Martinez muttered from his position near the ammo rack. "Feels like we're pushing our luck every day."

"We've made it this far," Tom "Wheels" Anderson said from the driver's seat. "We'll keep going. That's what we do."

Jack climbed down from the turret, landing heavily on the cobblestones below. He surveyed the area, taking in the faces of the soldiers and tank crews around him. These were men who had been through hell and back, and now they were being asked to push even further into enemy territory.

He climbed back into the tank and addressed the crew. "Alright, you heard the orders. Wheels, make sure the engine's ready for another long run. Grizzly, check the bow gun. Deadeye, clean the optics. Quick Hands, double-check our ammo load. We're not going into this half-prepared."

"On it, Boss," the crew replied in unison, their fatigue momentarily overridden by the familiar rhythm of preparation.

As they worked, the sounds of the camp swirled around them: the clatter of tools as mechanics worked on damaged tanks, the murmur of voices as officers coordinated the next moves, and the distant cries of the wounded being tended by medics. This was the reality of war—a relentless grind forward, no matter the cost.

Once the Iron Wolf was prepped, the crew settled in for a few stolen hours of rest. Inside the tank, the atmosphere was tense but resolute. Each man knew what lay ahead: more battles, more resistance, and more danger. But they also knew they had each other—and the Iron Wolf.

As the first light of dawn crept over the horizon, the camp came alive with activity. Engines roared to life, soldiers packed their gear, and the column began to assemble. The Iron Wolf moved into position near the front, its crew ready for whatever awaited them in the heart of Germany.

"Alright, boys," Jack said, his voice steady as the tank rolled forward. "This is it. We're going deeper than we've ever been. Stay sharp, watch each other's backs, and remember—this war doesn't end until we make it end."

The crew nodded, their expressions grim but determined. The Iron Wolf pressed on, leading the charge into the unknown. The road ahead would be perilous, but for the crew of the Iron Wolf, there was no turning back. The heart of Germany awaited, and they would face it together.

Chapter 12: The Final Campaign

The Iron Wolf advanced cautiously along a muddy road lined with shattered trees and bomb craters, its tracks grinding through the thick sludge. The heart of Germany was a grim and hostile landscape, and every inch was contested fiercely. The closer they pushed to Berlin, the more desperate and fanatical the resistance became.

"All units, be advised," crackled Lieutenant Parker's voice over the radio. "We're facing Waffen-SS and Hitler Youth in this sector. Expect heavy resistance and no chance of surrender. Watch yourselves."

Jack "Boss" Harris glanced at his crew, their expressions somber as the weight of the warning sank in. The Waffen-SS were infamous for their brutal tactics, and the thought of facing children—no matter how indoctrinated—was a chilling prospect.

"Grizzly, keep that bow gun ready," Jack ordered, his voice firm. "Deadeye, scan every inch of the road ahead. Wheels, keep us moving slow. Quick Hands, load solid shot—we're not taking any chances."

"Solid shot loaded," Joe "Quick Hands" Martinez replied, his voice tight with tension.

"Boss," George "Grizzly" Thompson said from the bow gun, his eyes fixed on the treeline. "You hear that? Sounds like movement up ahead."

The faint sound of voices and the rustle of leaves reached their ears, carried on the cold wind. Jack peered through the periscope, scanning the road ahead. A wooden barricade had been hastily constructed across the road, and figures darted behind it.

"Deadeye, target that barricade," Jack said. "Quick Hands, get a Boomer ready next. Grizzly, lay down suppressing fire."

"On it," Mike "Deadeye" Walker replied, swinging the turret toward the barricade.

George opened up with the bow gun, spraying the area with .30-caliber rounds. The figures behind the barricade scattered, but some returned fire, their bullets pinging harmlessly off the Sherman's armor. Through the periscope, Jack saw a young boy—no older than 14—firing a rifle with shaking hands.

"Christ, it's the Hitler Youth," George muttered, his voice filled with unease. "They've got kids out here."

"No time to think about it," Jack said grimly. "Deadeye, take out that barricade."

The cannon roared, the high-explosive shell slamming into the wooden structure. The barricade splintered into pieces, sending debris and bodies flying. The survivors scattered, disappearing into the treeline.

"Quick Hands, reload," Jack ordered. "Grizzly, keep scanning the flanks. Wheels, move us forward."

"Boomer reloaded," Joe said, his hands moving automatically.

The tank rolled forward, its turret sweeping the area as the crew remained on high alert. As they approached the destroyed barricade, a sudden burst of fire erupted from the treeline. Waffen-SS soldiers emerged, their camouflage uniforms blending into the foliage as they fired Panzerfausts and rifles.

"Panzerfaust, left side!" George shouted.

Tom "Wheels" Anderson reacted instantly, turning the tank to angle its armor. The Panzerfaust fired, the rocket streaking toward the Iron Wolf and striking its front armor with a deafening impact. The Sherman shuddered, but the round failed to penetrate.

"Deadeye, hit that treeline!" Jack yelled.

Mike fired, the high-explosive shell slamming into the dense foliage. The explosion tore through the German position, scattering bodies and leaving a smoking crater. George opened up with the bow gun, mowing down the remaining soldiers as they attempted to retreat.

"They're fanatics," Mike said grimly. "They'd rather die than surrender."

"Then we give them what they want," Jack replied coldly. "Quick Hands, reload. Wheels, keep us moving. We can't stop now."

As the Iron Wolf pressed deeper into the sector, the resistance grew more intense. Waffen-SS soldiers and Hitler Youth fought with a ferocity born of desperation, their tactics ruthless and unrelenting. For the crew of the Sherman, it was a grim reminder that the end of the war would be paid for in blood.

Inside the tank, the crew was silent, each man processing the horrors they were witnessing. They had fought through countless battles, but this was different. The fanatical resistance in the heart of Germany tested not only their skills but also their resolve.

The Iron Wolf pressed on, its tracks grinding through the mud and debris as it led the charge. For Jack and his crew, there was no turning back. This was the final campaign, and they were determined to see it through to the bitter end.

The Iron Wolf sat still on the battlefield, its engine idling as smoke drifted through the air. The skirmish had ended moments ago, leaving the road littered with debris and bodies. Among them, the lifeless figure of a young German soldier lay crumpled in the mud, his rifle still clutched in his hands. He couldn't have been more than sixteen, his face pale and expressionless in the dim light.

Inside the tank, the crew was silent, the weight of the moment pressing down on them like the steel walls around them. Jack "Boss" Harris peered through the periscope, his jaw tight as he scanned the aftermath.

"Kid didn't stand a chance," George "Grizzly" Thompson muttered from the bow gun. His hands rested on the controls, but he wasn't scanning for threats anymore. His eyes were fixed on the boy's body.

"It's war," Mike "Deadeye" Walker said, his voice flat but hollow. "They put a rifle in his hands and sent him out here. He made his choice."

"Did he, though?" Joe "Quick Hands" Martinez asked, leaning back against the ammo rack. His voice was quieter than usual, tinged with something close to regret. "He was a kid. Probably didn't even know what he was fighting for."

Jack exhaled, his hands gripping the turret ring. "We don't get to decide who they send to fight us," he said firmly. "That kid was holding a rifle and pointing it at our men. If we hesitated, it could've been one of us lying out there instead."

"But does that make it right?" Joe pressed, his voice rising slightly. "We're out here mowing down teenagers like they're enemy soldiers. Hell, they barely know what they're doing."

"It's not about right or wrong," Mike snapped. "It's about surviving. You think they'd hesitate if it was one of us? You think that kid wouldn't have pulled the trigger if he had the chance?"

Joe shook his head, his jaw tightening. "Doesn't mean it doesn't eat at you," he muttered.

Tom "Wheels" Anderson finally spoke, his voice calm but heavy. "I've been thinking about home lately," he said. "About my nephew. He's fourteen. Looks a lot like that kid out there. Can't stop wondering… what if it was him? What if it was my family fighting on the other side?"

The tank fell silent again, the weight of Tom's words settling over the crew like a fog. Outside, the battlefield was eerily quiet, the only sounds the distant crackle of fire and the occasional shout from advancing troops.

"War doesn't care about your family," Jack said finally, his tone firm but not unkind. "It doesn't care about right, or fair, or who deserves to live or die. It's ugly, and it's cruel, and it drags everyone down with it. But we're here to end it. Every step forward is a step closer to making sure kids like that don't have to fight again."

Joe looked down, his hands fidgeting with the strap on his helmet. "I get it, Boss. I do. But it doesn't make it any easier."

"It's not supposed to be easy," George said quietly. "If it was, we'd all be monsters."

Jack nodded, his gaze still fixed on the periscope. "We don't forget," he said. "We don't lose ourselves in this. But we do the job. We finish it."

The crew nodded, their faces grim but resolute. They knew the cost of war all too well, and every day it seemed to climb higher. But they also knew that stopping wasn't an option. The Iron Wolf rumbled back to life, its engine roaring as it pressed forward once more.

Outside, the young soldier's body faded into the distance, just another casualty in a war that demanded so much from everyone it touched. Inside the Sherman, the men carried his memory with them, a reminder of the human cost of the mission they were determined to see through to the end.

The Iron Wolf sat at the edge of a tree line, its engine idling as the crew prepared for what lay ahead. Through his periscope, Jack "Boss" Harris surveyed the battlefield: an open expanse of muddy fields, crisscrossed with barbed wire and pockmarked with craters from artillery strikes. Beyond it lay the target—a heavily fortified German position, bristling with machine guns, anti-tank weapons, and entrenched infantry.

"All units, this is Command," came the crackling voice of Lieutenant Parker over the radio. "This is the final push. That position has to fall. Tanks will lead the assault, infantry will follow. Expect heavy resistance. Good luck."

Jack keyed the mic. "Iron Wolf copies. We're ready."

Inside the tank, the tension was palpable. The crew knew what was coming—they had faced fortified positions before, and it was never easy. This time, though, the stakes felt higher. They were deep in enemy territory, and the Germans were fighting with the desperation of a force with nothing left to lose.

"Wheels, move us forward," Jack ordered. "Grizzly, keep the bow gun hot. Deadeye, get ready to fire as soon as you see a target. Quick Hands, load a Boomer."

"Boomer loaded," Joe "Quick Hands" Martinez confirmed, his hands moving with practiced efficiency.

The Iron Wolf rolled out of the treeline, its tracks churning through the mud as the platoon advanced. The other Shermans moved in a staggered formation, their turrets swiveling as they scanned for threats. Behind them, infantry huddled low, using the tanks as cover.

"Boss, they see us," George "Grizzly" Thompson muttered from the bow gun. "They're getting ready."

From the German lines, the crackle of rifle fire grew into a roar as machine guns opened up. Tracers streaked across the battlefield, slicing through the air like deadly ribbons. The first

Sherman in the column took a direct hit from an 88mm anti-tank gun, its turret exploding in a fireball. The crew inside had no chance.

"Damn it!" Jack shouted. "Deadeye, target that 88! Quick Hands, get a solid shot ready!"

"On target," Mike "Deadeye" Walker said, swinging the turret toward the enemy gun. He fired, and the Sherman's cannon roared. The high-explosive round struck the anti-tank position, obliterating the crew and sending shards of steel and dirt into the air.

"Solid shot loaded!" Joe called out.

"Keep moving!" Jack ordered. "Wheels, angle us toward that bunker on the right. Grizzly, cover the infantry!"

The Iron Wolf pressed forward, bullets pinging off its armor as George sprayed the enemy trenches with the bow gun. Allied infantry moved up alongside the tanks, but the fire from the German lines was relentless. Another Sherman was hit, its tracks blown apart by a mine. The crew bailed out, only to be cut down by machine-gun fire.

"Boss, that bunker's lighting us up!" Mike shouted, his voice strained.

Jack swung the periscope toward the bunker. Its machine guns were mowing down Allied troops, the gunners showing no mercy. "Deadeye, take it out!" he barked.

Mike adjusted his aim, his hands steady despite the chaos. "Firing!" he shouted.

The cannon roared again, the shell slamming into the bunker. The explosion blew apart the sandbags and sent the gunners flying, their bodies slamming against the walls before crumpling lifeless to the ground.

"Target neutralized," Mike reported, already lining up another shot.

The Iron Wolf rolled over the barbed wire, its tracks flattening the obstacles as it pushed closer to the German lines. The battlefield was a hellscape of fire and smoke, the screams of the wounded mixing with the deafening roar of gunfire and explosions.

"Boss, infantry's taking heavy losses!" George called out. "We're losing guys fast!"

Jack's jaw tightened. He knew the cost of this assault would be high, but seeing it unfold was something else entirely. "We've got to keep pushing," he said. "We take that position, or it's all for nothing."

The tank pressed on, its cannon and machine guns blazing as it tore through the German defenses. Around them, the other Shermans continued the assault, but their numbers were dwindling. Bodies littered the battlefield, both Allied and German, a grim testament to the ferocity of the fight.

Finally, the Iron Wolf reached the German lines, its cannon blasting the last of the defenders from their positions. The surviving infantry surged forward, clearing the trenches with grenades and close-quarters combat. The fortified position was theirs—but at a staggering cost.

Inside the tank, the crew was silent, their faces pale as they took in the aftermath. Smoke and fire filled the air, and the ground was slick with mud and blood. They had survived, but many of their comrades hadn't.

"Is it over?" Joe asked quietly, his voice trembling.

"For now," Jack replied, his voice heavy with exhaustion. "But it's not the end. Not yet."

The Iron Wolf sat idle as the remaining tanks and infantry regrouped. The position was secured, but the price of victory weighed heavily on everyone who had fought to claim it. For the crew of the Iron Wolf, the last push had been their hardest battle yet—but they knew the war wasn't done with them yet.

The Iron Wolf sat in the shadows of a ruined village, its engine idling softly as the crew gathered their nerves. Word had come down from command: a German Tiger tank was guarding a critical road leading deeper into Germany. The Tiger wasn't just a tank—it was a symbol of German engineering and power, feared by every Allied tanker who faced one. Its thick armor and devastating 88mm gun made it a lethal adversary, capable of destroying a Sherman from distances where the Sherman's rounds would bounce harmlessly off its hull.

"All units, be advised," came Lieutenant Parker's voice over the radio. "That road has to be ours. The Tiger is holding position near a chokepoint. Flank it, distract it, do whatever you have to do, but take it out. We cannot advance until it's destroyed. Good luck."

Jack "Boss" Harris turned to his crew, his face grim. "Alright, listen up. This isn't just another tank. The Tiger's gun can take us out with one shot, and its armor will laugh at anything but a Super round at the right angle. We don't fight this head-on. Wheels, we'll move through the ruins and try to get a flank. Deadeye, you're gonna have one shot, and it has to count. Quick Hands, keep those Supers ready. Grizzly, eyes on the flanks for infantry."

The crew nodded, their usual banter replaced by tense determination. This was the fight every tanker feared, and they knew the stakes.

"Solid plan, Boss," George "Grizzly" Thompson muttered. "Just don't ask me to trade places with Deadeye."

Mike "Deadeye" Walker cracked a faint grin, though his eyes remained locked on the gun sights. "Don't worry, Grizz. I'll do the hard part."

"Let's make sure he gets the chance," Tom "Wheels" Anderson said from the driver's seat, his hands gripping the controls tightly.

Joe "Quick Hands" Martinez checked the ammunition racks, his fingers trembling slightly as he loaded the Super HVAP round. "Super loaded," he said, his voice steady despite the tension.

Jack keyed the mic. "Iron Wolf moving out."

The Sherman rolled slowly through the ruins, its tracks crunching over debris as the crew kept their eyes peeled for any sign of the Tiger. The village was eerily quiet, the stillness broken only by the faint crackle of distant fires and the occasional distant gunshot. Every shadow seemed to hold danger, every corner a potential ambush.

"Boss, I've got movement," Mike said, his voice low. "Dead ahead, about two hundred yards."

Jack swung the periscope toward the road. There it was: the Tiger. Its massive hull sat at the chokepoint, partially concealed by rubble and a twisted metal barricade. The long barrel of its 88mm gun scanned the area slowly, a predator waiting for prey.

"There's our target," Jack said. "Wheels, take us left, through those buildings. We'll flank it."

The Iron Wolf moved carefully, its engine rumbling softly as it weaved through the narrow alleys of the ruined village. The crew held their breath, every creak of the tank's hull sounding impossibly loud. They knew that if the Tiger spotted them, it would only take one shot to end everything.

"Boss, we've got infantry moving near the Tiger," George said. "Looks like they're covering it."

"Grizzly, keep an eye on them, but don't fire unless they spot us," Jack ordered. "We can't give away our position."

As the Sherman edged closer, the Tiger remained focused on the main road, unaware of the Iron Wolf's approach. Jack's heart pounded in his chest as he directed the tank into position. "Deadeye, get ready," he said. "We've got one shot at this."

Mike adjusted the gun sights, lining up the Tiger's side armor. "Got it," he said, his voice steady.

"Quick Hands, Super loaded?" Jack asked.

"Super's ready," Joe replied, his hands gripping the shell loader tightly.

"Wheels, hold steady," Jack said. "Deadeye, aim for the engine compartment. When I give the word, fire."

The Iron Wolf settled into position, its crew tense but focused. The Tiger loomed ahead, oblivious to the Sherman's presence. Jack took a deep breath, his fingers hovering over the intercom switch.

"Now," he said.

The Sherman's cannon roared, the HVAP round streaking across the battlefield and slamming into the Tiger's side. The tungsten core punched through the armor, hitting the engine compartment. Flames erupted from the rear of the Tiger, black smoke pouring into the sky.

The German tank's turret began to turn, but it was too late. The fire spread rapidly, and the crew inside bailed out, their uniforms ablaze. George opened up with the bow gun, cutting down the fleeing soldiers as the Tiger burned.

"Target destroyed!" Mike called, his voice tinged with relief.

"Good work," Jack said, exhaling slowly. "Quick Hands, reload. Grizzly, watch for counterattacks. Wheels, keep us moving—don't let us become a sitting target."

The Iron Wolf pulled back into cover as the flames consumed the Tiger. The road was clear, but the crew knew the fight wasn't over yet. They had taken down one of the most fearsome weapons in the German arsenal, but the road ahead would only get harder.

Inside the Sherman, the men exchanged weary glances, the weight of their victory tempered by the knowledge of what still lay ahead.

"That was too close," Joe said, his hands still trembling slightly.

"It always is," Jack replied. "But we did it. Now let's keep moving. We're not done yet."

The Iron Wolf rolled slowly through the rubble-strewn streets, its engine rumbling like a low growl. The air was heavy with smoke and tension as the crew prepared to face the deadliest foe they had yet encountered: the German Tiger tank. The Sherman's hull creaked under the strain of movement, every sound amplified in the oppressive silence that surrounded them.

"Deadeye, you've got one shot at this," Jack "Boss" Harris said, his voice steady but taut. "Make it count."

"Understood," Mike "Deadeye" Walker replied, his hands gripping the gun controls tightly.

"Quick Hands, Super round ready?" Jack asked.

Joe "Quick Hands" Martinez held the tungsten-cored HVAP round in his hands, the weight of it somehow heavier than any before. "Super loaded," he said, sliding the shell into the breech and slamming it shut.

"Grizzly, eyes on the flanks. No surprises," Jack continued. "Wheels, keep us slow and steady. We don't want to spook it."

Tom "Wheels" Anderson nodded, his knuckles white on the controls. "Got it, Boss."

The Tiger sat in a strategic position, its massive gun pointed down the main road. The German tank seemed like a sleeping beast, its angular hull and long barrel a terrifying silhouette against the smoke-filled horizon. The Iron Wolf had managed to flank it, moving through the ruins to approach its vulnerable side, but the challenge was far from over.

"Boss, I see infantry near the Tiger," George "Grizzly" Thompson said from the bow gun. "They're watching its back."

"Keep your fire tight," Jack ordered. "We don't want to draw attention until Deadeye's got the shot."

The Iron Wolf crept closer, the crew holding their breath as they approached the Tiger's blind spot. Through the periscope, Jack could see the enemy tank's exhaust pouring faint plumes of smoke into the cold air. It hadn't spotted them yet, but one wrong move would change that in an instant.

"Deadeye, target the engine compartment," Jack said. "It's the only spot we've got a chance of penetrating."

"On target," Mike replied, his voice calm despite the tension. He adjusted the sights, lining up the shot with painstaking precision. The Tiger's thick armor was impenetrable from most angles, but the rear engine compartment was its Achilles' heel—if he could hit it.

"Wheels, hold position," Jack said. "Quick Hands, stay ready to reload if we need another shot."

The Sherman came to a halt, its engine idling as the crew prepared for the moment of truth. The seconds stretched into eternity, each man's heart pounding in his chest.

"Fire!" Jack ordered.

The cannon roared, the HVAP round streaking toward the Tiger with deadly precision. The tungsten core struck the rear of the German tank, punching through the armor and into the engine compartment. A split second later, the Tiger erupted in flames, a thunderous explosion tearing through its hull. Black smoke poured into the sky as the beast was finally slain.

The German crew scrambled to escape, their uniforms ablaze. George opened up with the bow gun, cutting them down before they could regroup. The battlefield fell silent once more, the only sound the crackling of the burning Tiger.

"Target destroyed," Mike said, his voice filled with relief and exhaustion.

"Good work," Jack said, his voice steady despite the adrenaline coursing through him. "Quick Hands, reload. Grizzly, watch for infantry. Wheels, let's move—we don't stay in one place after a shot like that."

The Iron Wolf pulled back into the cover of the ruins, its engine rumbling like a satisfied predator. The Tiger was no more, its charred wreckage a stark reminder of the crew's resolve and skill. Inside the Sherman, the men exchanged glances, their relief tempered by the knowledge that the war was still far from over.

"That was the toughest one yet," Joe said quietly, his hands still trembling slightly as he handled the next round.

"Yeah," Tom replied, his voice heavy. "But we did it. We took it down."

"We'll take down whatever else they throw at us," Jack said firmly. "We've come too far to stop now."

The Iron Wolf pressed on, leaving the burning wreckage of the Tiger behind. For the crew, the victory was bittersweet—another step forward in a war that demanded everything from them. But as the tank moved deeper into Germany, they knew they were closer than ever to the end.

Chapter 13: War's End

The Iron Wolf sat idle in a quiet German field, its hull streaked with mud and smoke, a testament to the brutal campaign it had survived. The air was still, a strange calm settling over the battlefield. Jack "Boss" Harris leaned against the turret ring, his helmet resting in his lap as he scanned the horizon through tired eyes. The war was over. The announcement had come through the radio earlier that day: Germany had surrendered.

"All units, this is Command," the radio had crackled. "The war in Europe is over. Stand down. Await further orders for regrouping and debriefing. You did it. We did it. Stand proud."

But the crew of the Iron Wolf didn't feel like celebrating. The price of victory had been staggering, and the scars left by the war—both physical and emotional—ran deep.

Inside the tank, the mood was somber. George "Grizzly" Thompson sat silently at the bow gun, his hands resting on the controls. Tom "Wheels" Anderson leaned back in the driver's seat, staring at nothing in particular. Mike "Deadeye" Walker cleaned the gun sights with methodical precision, while Joe "Quick Hands" Martinez sat near the ammo rack, his hands fidgeting with a spent shell casing.

"We made it," Joe said quietly, his voice breaking the silence. "The war's over. We should be happy, right?"

George snorted softly, shaking his head. "Happy? For what? We've been through hell, and half the guys we started with didn't make it."

"More than half," Mike muttered, his voice heavy. "Charlie, Parker, the boys from the other platoons... hell, I don't even know how many names we've lost."

Jack climbed down from the turret, landing heavily on the ground beside the tank. He glanced at the men inside, their faces pale and drawn. "We did our job," he said firmly, though his tone lacked its usual confidence. "We fought so they didn't have to. That has to mean something."

"Does it, though?" Tom asked, his voice quiet but filled with doubt. "I keep thinking about the ones we couldn't save. The civilians, the kids... even some of the Krauts we fought. Feels like we lost pieces of ourselves out here."

Jack nodded slowly, his gaze drifting toward the horizon. "We did," he admitted. "But we kept going. We had to. That's the cost of war."

The crew fell silent again, each man lost in his own thoughts. The battlefield around them was eerily peaceful, a stark contrast to the chaos they had endured. The wreckage of burned-out tanks and abandoned weapons littered the landscape, a grim reminder of the price they had paid for this moment.

"We made it through," Joe said finally, his voice tinged with both relief and sorrow. "Not all of us, but we did."

"Yeah," George said softly. "But at what cost?"

Jack glanced at him, his expression unreadable. "At the cost of a future where maybe the next generation won't have to fight like this," he said. "That's what we fought for. That's why it matters."

The crew nodded slowly, the weight of Jack's words settling over them. They had endured horrors they could never forget, but they had also accomplished something few could claim: they had survived, and they had won.

As the sun dipped lower in the sky, casting long shadows across the field, the Iron Wolf stood as a silent sentinel—a testament to the men who had fought and bled to bring the war to an end. The battle was over, but the memories would stay with them forever. For Jack and his crew, victory came at a cost they would carry for the rest of their lives.

Part 2: Reflection and Farewell

The crew of the Iron Wolf sat together on the cold steel of their tank, the quiet of the evening wrapping around them like a heavy blanket. For the first time in months, there was no urgency to move, no orders to follow, and no enemy to fight. The war was over, but the silence wasn't peaceful—it was heavy with the weight of loss.

Jack "Boss" Harris pulled a crumpled envelope from his jacket pocket, his fingers lingering over the faded ink. The letter had been passed to him by a courier earlier that day, delivered from a stateside family. It bore the name of Charlie, their friend and fellow tanker who had died in the Ardennes.

"Got this today," Jack said softly, holding the letter up for the crew to see. "From Charlie's folks."

The men fell silent, their attention shifting to Jack. The mention of Charlie brought a fresh wave of emotion to the surface. He had been one of them—a friend, a brother-in-arms, and a reminder of the fragility of their lives out here.

Jack unfolded the letter carefully, the paper worn from its journey. Clearing his throat, he began to read.

"Dear Sirs,

I'm writing this letter in the hope that someone from my boy's unit might read it. Charlie always spoke about his crew like they were family, and I thought you should know how proud we are of him. He told us stories about all of you, about the Iron Wolf, and about the things you've been through together.

We got word of his passing last month. It broke our hearts, but it also reminded us of the kind of man Charlie was. Brave, loyal, and always looking out for others. If it weren't for you, I think he would have been lost out there. You gave him a purpose, and for that, we're grateful.

I just wanted to say thank you. You were his brothers, and I hope you make it home safe. Charlie would've wanted that. Please remember him, not for how he left, but for how he lived—with courage and heart.

God bless you all,

Mrs. Margaret Langford."

Jack's voice cracked slightly as he finished reading, his eyes scanning the faces of his crew. George "Grizzly" Thompson looked down at his hands, his jaw tight as he blinked back tears. Tom "Wheels" Anderson leaned back against the tank, his face pale as he let out a shaky breath.

Mike "Deadeye" Walker stared into the distance, his lips pressed into a thin line. Joe "Quick Hands" Martinez wiped his face with the back of his hand, his composure slipping.

"He was a good man," George said quietly. "Damn good."

Jack folded the letter and tucked it back into his pocket. "He was one of us," he said firmly. "And we'll never forget him. None of us."

The crew nodded, their silence more powerful than any words. For months, they had been focused on survival, burying their grief under layers of duty and adrenaline. Now, with the war over, there was nothing to distract them from the losses they had endured.

"Think his family will ever really understand what he went through?" Tom asked, his voice soft.

Jack shook his head. "I don't think anyone back home can truly understand. But they don't have to. They just need to know he fought for something bigger than himself—and that he didn't die alone."

The men sat together as the sun dipped below the horizon, the letter a stark reminder of the humanity they had fought to protect and the lives they had left behind. Charlie's memory wasn't just a name or a story—it was a bond they carried with them, a reminder of what they had survived and why they had fought.

For the crew of the Iron Wolf, the war was over, but the weight of their experiences—and the memory of their fallen comrades—would stay with them forever. As the night deepened, they shared quiet stories about Charlie, their voices mingling with the rustle of the wind and the distant hum of the post-war world awakening around them.

The Iron Wolf sat silent in a makeshift depot, its battle-worn hull finally at rest. Around it, soldiers packed up their gear, awaiting transport back to their respective countries. The war in Europe was over, and for the first time in years, Jack and his crew faced a future beyond the battlefield. Yet, the weight of what they had endured—and survived—hung heavy in the air.

"Feels weird, doesn't it?" George "Grizzly" Thompson said, breaking the silence. He leaned against the Sherman's side, staring at the departing convoys with a distant expression. "Packing up, heading home... like we're just supposed to forget everything."

Jack "Boss" Harris stood nearby, his arms crossed as he watched the activity around them. "We're not supposed to forget," he said quietly. "We're just supposed to keep going."

Tom "Wheels" Anderson was sitting on a crate near the tank's tracks, running a hand through his unkempt hair. "I keep thinking about the guys who didn't make it," he said, his voice low. "Charlie, Parker, the other crews... they're not going home. Feels like we're leaving them behind."

"You're not leaving them behind," Mike "Deadeye" Walker said, his tone sharp but filled with emotion. "They're coming with us, every damn step of the way. You think you're ever going to forget Charlie cracking jokes during downtime? Or Parker pulling us out of that ditch back in the Ardennes? They're part of us now."

Joe "Quick Hands" Martinez nodded, his hands fidgeting with the edge of his duffle bag. "Deadeye's right," he said. "But it doesn't stop it from hurting. Doesn't stop me from wondering why we're here and they're not."

Jack sighed, stepping forward to address his crew. "Survivor's guilt," he said plainly. "We all have it. It's the price we pay for making it out when others didn't. But guilt doesn't help anyone. The best thing we can do for them—for all of them—is to live. To go home, remember their names, and build something worth all the sacrifices we made."

The crew fell silent, Jack's words settling over them like the cool evening air. Around them, the depot bustled with soldiers eager to leave, their faces a mix of relief and apprehension. For many, returning home was almost as daunting as the war itself.

"What do you think it's going to be like?" Joe asked suddenly. "Going home, I mean. After all this."

Jack thought for a moment before answering. "Different," he said honestly. "We've changed. The world's changed. It's not going to be easy, but we've got to try. That's the whole point of what we fought for, isn't it? To give ourselves and the people back home a chance to start over."

Tom looked up at the tank, its battered hull a symbol of everything they'd been through. "What about her?" he asked. "What happens to the Iron Wolf?"

"She stays here," Jack said, his voice heavy with emotion. "She did her job. She got us through this war. Now she gets to rest, too."

The crew nodded, their gazes lingering on the Sherman that had been their home and shield through the darkest days of their lives. The Iron Wolf was more than just a machine—it was a part of their story, a silent witness to their struggles and victories.

As the sun began to set, casting a warm glow over the depot, the crew gathered their belongings and prepared for the journey home. Each man carried more than just his gear—he carried the memories, the scars, and the bonds forged in the crucible of war.

"Alright," Jack said, his voice steady but filled with emotion. "Let's go home."

The men exchanged quiet glances, each one filled with unspoken understanding. They had survived together, and now they would return to a world that might not understand what they had been through. But they would face it, just as they had faced every challenge before.

As they walked away from the Iron Wolf, its silhouette stood against the fading light—a symbol of their resilience and the price they had paid for peace.

The train station buzzed with the muted activity of soldiers waiting to board, their faces a mix of exhaustion and anticipation. Jack "Boss" Harris and the crew of the Iron Wolf stood together near a weathered bench, their bags at their feet, as they prepared to part ways for the first time since the war began. The realization was heavy: this was the end of their journey together.

George "Grizzly" Thompson adjusted the straps of his duffle bag, his usual grin absent. "This is it, huh?" he said, breaking the silence. "The Iron Wolves breaking up for good."

"Feels strange," Joe "Quick Hands" Martinez replied, his voice subdued. "After everything we've been through... just walking away like this."

Mike "Deadeye" Walker sat on the bench, his rifle balanced across his knees. "We've done our job," he said firmly. "And now it's time to go home. But yeah... it feels wrong leaving it all behind."

Tom "Wheels" Anderson leaned against a nearby post, staring down the length of the train tracks. "Never thought I'd say this," he muttered, "but I'm gonna miss you guys."

Jack nodded, his arms crossed as he surveyed the group. "We're all gonna miss this," he said, his voice steady. "Not the war, not the killing—but this. Us. What we had in that tank."

The crew fell silent, each man grappling with the weight of Jack's words. The bond they had forged in the Iron Wolf was unlike anything else, built on trust, sacrifice, and the shared experience of surviving the worst humanity had to offer.

George broke the silence with a chuckle, though it lacked its usual humor. "You know," he said, "I always thought Grizzly's Lucky Coin would see us through to the end. Guess it worked."

He flipped the battered coin into the air, catching it with a grin that didn't quite reach his eyes. "Guess I'll keep it for good luck on the next chapter."

"You'd better," Jack said with a smirk. "I don't think any of us would have made it without that damn thing."

Joe shook his head, a faint smile crossing his face. "What do we even do now? Go home and pretend none of this ever happened?"

"No," Jack said firmly. "We don't pretend. We carry it with us. Everything we've been through, everything we've lost—it's part of who we are now. But we don't let it drag us down. We live."

Tom looked at the others, his gaze lingering on each of them. "Think we'll ever see each other again?"

Jack hesitated before answering. "Maybe," he said quietly. "But maybe not. Doesn't change what we've got, though. We'll always be Iron Wolves. That's not something time or distance can take away."

The train whistle blew, signaling its arrival. The crew exchanged glances, the moment they had been dreading finally at hand. One by one, they stepped forward, shaking hands, clapping each other on the shoulders, and exchanging quiet words of farewell.

"Take care of yourself, Deadeye," George said, his usual teasing tone replaced with genuine warmth.

"You too, Grizz," Mike replied. "Try not to get into too much trouble."

Joe hugged Tom briefly, his voice shaky as he said, "Thanks for getting us through all that, Wheels. You kept us alive."

Tom smiled faintly. "Just doing my part, Quick Hands. Keep your head on straight out there."

Finally, Jack addressed the group, his voice filled with quiet authority. "You're all more than just soldiers. You're my brothers. No matter where life takes us, no matter how far apart we end up, that doesn't change. You hear me?"

The crew nodded, their emotions raw as they said their final goodbyes. The train pulled into the station, its brakes screeching as it came to a halt. Jack watched as his crew boarded, each man taking his place in one of the passenger cars. He was the last to step on, turning briefly to look back at the platform.

The Iron Wolf was gone, left behind on a battlefield that would eventually fade into history. But the memories of what they had endured together would stay with them forever.

As the train began to move, Jack took his seat and gazed out the window. The faces of his crew lingered in his mind, their bond unbroken despite the miles that would soon separate them. They were no longer just soldiers—they were survivors, brothers, and the last of the Iron Wolves.

The rhythmic clatter of train wheels filled the quiet cabin as the countryside blurred past the window. Jack "Boss" Harris sat alone, his duffle bag tucked at his feet, and the worn envelope containing Charlie's letter clutched in his hand. Outside, the rolling hills and quiet villages seemed untouched by the devastation of war—a stark contrast to the memories that played out endlessly in his mind.

Jack leaned back, staring out at the peaceful horizon. The war was over, but it felt far from behind him. Every mile the train traveled, every town they passed, seemed to carry echoes of the men who wouldn't be returning home. The faces of his crew, the brothers he had fought alongside, were etched into his thoughts. The bond they had forged in the Iron Wolf had been forged in blood and fire—a bond that no distance could break.

He pulled out Charlie's letter and unfolded it, rereading the words he had read so many times before. Mrs. Langford's gratitude for their bond, her pride in her son's bravery, was a bittersweet comfort. It reminded him of why they had fought—not for glory, but for each other and the people they had left behind.

"Charlie, Parker, all of you," Jack murmured, his voice barely above a whisper. "You deserved better than this."

He thought about the tank itself, the Iron Wolf. It had been their shield, their weapon, and their home. More than a machine, it had carried their hopes, fears, and lives through the darkest days of the war. Now, it sat abandoned in Germany, its job finished. But its legacy, like the men who had fought inside it, would endure.

Jack glanced around the train cabin. Other soldiers sat quietly, their faces reflecting a mix of exhaustion and anticipation. Some stared out the windows, while others wrote letters or simply sat in silence. Each man carried his own weight, his own stories of survival and sacrifice.

For Jack, the weight was heavier than he could have imagined. He thought of the countless lives lost—not just those of his crew but the enemy soldiers and civilians caught in the crossfire. The faces of the Hitler Youth, the Waffen-SS, and the shattered families they had encountered all blurred together, a stark reminder of the cost of war.

But even in the darkness, there was a sliver of hope. The sacrifices they had made, the pain they had endured, had led to this moment—a chance for peace. A chance for those who survived to rebuild and honor the memories of those who hadn't.

Jack reached into his jacket pocket and pulled out Grizzly's Lucky Coin, the small trinket that had been a talisman for their survival. He turned it over in his fingers, the worn edges smooth against his skin. It wasn't just a coin anymore—it was a symbol of everything they had endured and overcome.

"I'll carry you with me," he said softly, his voice resolute. "All of you. The Iron Wolf, the battles, the men we lost—you'll never be forgotten. Not while I'm still breathing."

The train whistle blew, signaling their approach to the station. Jack folded the letter carefully and placed it back in his pocket, along with the coin. As the train slowed, the quiet hum of anticipation filled the cabin. For the first time in years, they were going home.

As Jack stepped off the train and into the bustling station, the noise and movement around him felt almost overwhelming. Families embraced returning soldiers, their cries of joy mixing with the somber quiet of those who had no one waiting for them. Jack stood still for a moment, taking it all in.

He adjusted his duffle bag on his shoulder and began to walk, his mind filled with memories of the Iron Wolf and its crew. Their journey had been brutal, but it had also been filled with courage, loyalty, and sacrifice. They had been more than soldiers—they had been Iron Wolves, a brotherhood forged in the crucible of war.

Jack vowed to honor their legacy, to remember their stories, and to ensure that their sacrifices had not been in vain. The Iron Wolves might have disbanded, but their spirit would live on in him—and in the peace they had fought so hard to achieve.